LICK

CATNIP ASSASSINS BOOK FIVE

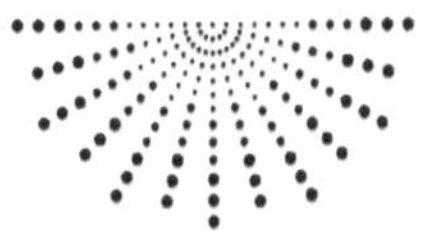

SKYE MACKINNON

Peryton Press

Cover by Ravenborn Covers.

Published by Peryton Press.

skyemackinnon.com

A QUICK WORD BEFORE WE GET STARTED

As you will know from the previous three books, this series is set in a world very similar to our own, but there are some deciding differences. Technology has developed differently, and while there are many devices you may be used to, such as televisions, there are no mobile phones, cars or the internet. No guns, either.

This book is written in British English and uses some British expressions and idioms. Please don't see these as spelling mistakes. We say mum rather than mom, use a lot of 's' instead of 'z' (cosy, realise, …) and use 'got' as the past participle of 'get' (instead of 'gotten').

And finally, subscribe to Skye's newsletter for updates about new releases:

skyemackinnon.com/newsletter.

You'll even get a free book for subscribing, so it's totally worth it.

WHAT HAPPENED BEFORE

Kat is an assassin who runs M.E.O.W. together with her friends Lily (half-succubus), Bethany (poisons expert) and Benjamin (thief). She has taken three mates: Lennox (a werewolf), Gryphon (a siren) and Ryker (a cat shifter).

Kat is one of ten clones, with her being the oldest. They were created by sirens controlling the Pack, in which she was trained as an assassin.

She's only met four of her clones: Ivy, Four, Caitlin and Little Kat. She's been told that only one other, K7, is still alive. Finding her lost sister is Kat's new priority after moving to Attenburgh for a new start. With them is Kat's sister/clone, Caitlin.

You thought it was over? You were wrong.

Kat is broke, so when she's offered a job as the mayor's bodyguard, she can't resist. It seems a simple enough job, until someone tries to kill her rather than the mayor.

At the same time, an incredibly valuable diamond needs to be stolen, a little deer needs a new home and there's a ball to attend.

When you put a cat in a dress, you should prepare for carnage…

CHAPTER ONE

Kittens are inherently evil. One minute, they look at you with big, heart-melting eyes, the next they try to cut your throat. Or bite a chunk out of your shoulder, in this case.

I grab the tabby by the scruff of its neck and throw it further down the bed. I was having such a good dream, one of knives and catnip. The kitten woke me and for that, it's going to pay.

"I'm going to tell Benjamin not to empty your litter tray," I announce with a yawn.

In response, the kitten sends me a mental image of it peeing on my beautiful new desk.

I almost throw a pillow at it. Did I mention that kittens are evil?

"Go back to sleep," Ryker mutters. "It's far too early."

"I would still be sleeping if this little devil hadn't woken me."

Ryker opens one eye, then closes it again. "That's Teapot. She's hungry."

"So? I'm hungry too, but that doesn't mean I go around biting people."

"You sure? You did a lot of biting last night."

I bare my teeth at him. "If I remember correctly, you enjoyed that. A lot."

"I'm not sure I remember…care to do it again?"

This time, I really do throw my pillow, but not at the kitten.

"Ouch!"

I roll my eyes. "It's a pillow, not a knife. Pillows are soft and don't hurt. Not unless you use them to suffocate someone. I've heard that can be a little painful."

"Thanks for the assassin lesson."

"Anytime." I sigh. "Now that we're both awake, how about breakfast?"

The kitten meows. I bare my teeth at it. "Not for you. You're going on the naughty step."

"We don't have a naughty step," Ryker reminds me.

"Then we'll introduce one. Although, I guess that would mean that our entire cat population would end up sitting on the stairs. That's a trip hazard."

Ryker laughs. "Your parenting skills still need to develop. I've heard you've taught Pumpkin how to detect different poisons?"

I shrug. "He needs to be prepared. If he ever shifts into a human, he'll need life skills. He's already good at hunting and overpowering prey, but he's still got a lot to learn."

Now that we all live in the same house, Pumpkin has been shadowing me constantly. He seems obsessed with my work and keeps asking for explanations of why and how I do things. Once, I caught him trying to walk on his hind legs. It almost broke my cold assassin heart.

Not that it's that cold any longer. My heart has thawed in the presence of my friends and males. And my family, even though only Caitlin is currently living with us. I got a letter from Ivy and Four yesterday though, and Little Kat regularly calls me. All three of them seem happy staying with Aunt Rose, although I bet that once the six months are up, I'm going to have to have a conversation with the twins. They still want to join me here. Rose has told me how well they're doing at school, so I really want them to stay with her. They can have a childhood there, but not here. Just because we have a bunch of kittens living with us doesn't mean that our home is suitable for adolescents. Especially not when they're about to start puberty. No thanks.

I stretch and climb out of bed. It's the biggest bed we could find, yet it's still a little small when all four of us are in it together. That doesn't happen very often though. As much as I love the three males, I do need time to myself. Cuddling is fine, but sometimes, I get claustrophobic when they surround me in my bed. I'm a cat and I need my independence.

Luckily, they all respect that. Every one of us has their own room, plus this one where we can all conglomerate when we feel like it. Last night, Gryphon had joined us, but he'd left in the early hours of the morning. Lennox is probably naked in a ditch somewhere. I grin at the image. It's a full moon and he's gone to the countryside to let his wolf enjoy some crazed howling and hunting.

Back home, a full moon was the time of the month when everyone would lock their doors at night and stay inside, wary of the shifters roaming the streets. Here in Attenburgh, it's very different. Shifters don't go out in public. Some days, I'm not even sure if humans know of our existence. For now, both Lennox and I have been careful with shifting outside. It's easy for Ryker, since he's not much larger than a normal cat when shifted, but a wolf and panther would definitely stand out. It's why Lennox is spending the full moon away from Attenburgh. I would have joined him, but I've got an important appointment today.

I check my watch. As much as it hurts to admit it, I'm glad the kitten woke me. I would have overslept otherwise.

To my annoyance – and envy – Ryker stays in bed. Lucky bastard.

I slowly make my way down to the first floor, where our living area is located. On the ground floor is my office, a lab and a weapon's storage. My favourite room in the entire house. The second floor is reserved for bedrooms and two baths. We don't have an attic though, at least not one as big as the one I used to live in. I miss my hammock, but I've conceded that it wouldn't be practical with having mates.

Our current attic is only two feet high, so we only use it for storage. If we ever have bodies to hide, it would be the perfect place. A little obvious though, perhaps.

Someone's left a plate of sandwiches on the counter. The rest of the M.E.O.W. team live in an outbuilding, but they don't have a kitchen over there, so we all use this one. It's nice to have the house just for family. My mates, my sister and me. Lily is out most of the time anyway, making friends with the locals. Which means fucking them and feeding off them. Even though she's only half-succubus, she's admitted that having sex gives her a sort of high. She doesn't need it, not like full succubi for whom it is essential to feed regularly. For Lily, it's just a nice side-effect of doing what she's good at. She's already provided us with a lot of information on how the upper class lives here. If what we've been told is correct, most members of Attenburgh's high society are sirens or at least in the employ of sirens.

Since we want to keep a low profile, Gryphon has been

staying home. He doesn't want to be recognised. It's been years since he last visited the city, but his father is fairly important and according to him, there's a clear family resemblance. Until we know more, it's better for him to stay hidden, no matter how much that irks him. He goes for walks at dawn or dusk, when it's still dark and the streets are empty. Luckily, we live in the outskirts of the city. It's the only part where we were able to afford a house like this. Rose's daughter, an estate agent, found it for us and got us an amazing price. For now, it's rented, until we decide whether we're going to make Attenburgh our permanent home or whether we'll move on once we've found my sister.

K7. The only sister I haven't found yet. She's somewhere in this city, if our sources are to be believed, but no matter how often Caitlin and I comb the streets on the hunt for her scent, we've been unsuccessful so far. Supposedly, K7 is feral at times, so it would make sense for her to be kept inside. I don't want to think of the possibility of her being kept in a facility or worse. No, in my mind, she's in a loving family who love her and keep her safe. It's a delusion, I know, but it's the only way I can keep a clear head when thinking of her.

I lean against the counter while munching on my sandwich. The bread has got a little moist from the gherkins inside, but I don't mind. It's food, that's what counts. I'm not much of a connoisseur. I can appreciate a good meal, but most of the time, I only eat something quick while my mind is on other things. Like right now.

I'm trying to remember what I've got planned for today. I'm too lazy to go downstairs into the office to check my to-do list. We have barely any clients here, not while trying to lay low, but for now, we have enough money. I don't need to find work right away. Still, I feel useless without at least a few marks on my list. I could randomly choose some people to kill, but that would make me a murderer and I prefer to be an assassin. I don't kill for fun. At least, not just. It's a business and I run it like one. With accounts and files and employees.

The sound of the cat flap opening makes me turn around. Ben installed it to make it easier for his horde of kittens to come and go as they please. A lot of Ryker's feline flock stayed behind, but at my last count, we still had twenty-one cats under his protection. Benjamin has taken on the role to look after the kittens, while Ryker makes sure the adults don't get themselves in trouble with the local cat population. There were a lot of battles for dominance at the beginning, but things seem to have calmed down. Soon, the cats will know Attenburgh as well as they did their old home, and they'll be able to spy and explore for me again. It's worth the massive amount of cat food that we have to buy every two weeks. And my catnip supply is under lock and key. I've given Pumpkin a tiny bit, but only once, since his father wasn't exactly pleased to find his son doing somersaults in the bathtub. If I have to choose between keeping Pumpkin or Ryker happy, then I'll always choose my Ryker.

Meow.

Speak of the kitten. Pumpkin enters the kitchen, his tail waving arrogantly from side to side. He's the ruler of the kittens and he's quickly taken to the role.

"Morning," I mutter while chewing on my last bite of sandwich.

Pumpkin meows before rubbing against my legs. I bend down to scratch his little head. He's still tiny, despite being close to feline adolescence. I wonder if he'll be small if he ever shifts. For now, all we can do is wait to see what happens with him.

"Your dad is upstairs, if you're looking for him," I tell Pumpkin when he turns his head to look around the kitchen, as if he's searching for something.

He sends me an image of the bag of catnip I keep stashed away.

"No. Not after last time. Ryker would kill me if I gave you any."

He looks up at me, his eyes seemingly growing bigger and cuter. I can almost hear my heart melt, turning into sticky drops.

No. I have to stay strong. I won't let a kitten tell me what to do. No matter how adorable he is.

"I won't give you catnip. But how about some milk? Or I'm sure there's a nice piece of steak in the fridge. Benjamin keeps it well stocked." He buys more food for the cats than for humans. Bethany has got angry more than once when he forgot to get snacks for her. She lives on snacks and junk food.

Pumpkin meows in protest. Spoilt little brat.

"I'm not going to budge. You can either have proper food now, or you can go away."

He glares at me, all cuteness gone. With a flick of his raised tail, he marches from the kitchen, leaving me feeling like an evil stepmother.

CHAPTER TWO

Someone's put a letter on my desk. It's more of a table than a proper desk, not like the beautiful old furniture I had back in Mystery Man's house. That's what I've decided to call him. Not his real name. That one is associated with too many bad memories.

I sit on my wooden chair - again lamenting the loss of my comfy leather office chair - and slice open the envelope. It's thick, high-quality paper, not the thin stuff you get in normal shops.

It's addressed to 'Dear Sir or Madam' and while I read through the text, I get the feeling that this is a generic letter, not one specifically written to me.

You are cordially invited to get involved in the business opportunity of the century. Riches beyond what you can imagine. The thrill of a once-in-a-lifetime adventure that could improve or take your life. Yes, this venture could be deadly, but the rewards are worth it. *

To find out more about this exclusive opportunity, please follow the hints provided. You will understand that we can only supply the most capable candidates of further details. Only attempt these trials if you have experience in subterfuge, stealth, theft, assassination or similar skills.

Please refrain from handing this letter to the police. Every letter has been marked and we will find out who broke confidentiality.

Sincerely,

The Widow

**in our opinion*

I read the letter several times. It didn't make much sense. Business opportunity of a lifetime. Now that sounded like something I could get behind on. Especially since I didn't have anything better to do.

How have they even found me though? I haven't exactly broadcast my presence in Attenburgh. Maybe it's some kind of spam mail that every household gets? No, the paper alone would cost too much for that to be viable. Someone knows I'm here, that *we* are here. It both pleases and worries me. Laying low isn't for me. I need something to do. This sounds better than staying here, twiddling my paws.

Follow the hints provided. I check the envelope, but there's nothing else inside, just the letter. Weird. Of course, there's no sender address on it either. That would have been far too easy.

I'm missing something. Unless they've forgotten to include the hints in my letter.

I grab it and its envelope and go on the search for whoever put the letter on my desk. I find Bethany in the living room, lazily flipping through a magazine. She barely glances up from it when I enter. I think she's a little bored too. I've not been able to give her a corpse to play with, nor has she needed to steal something or make new poisons. With Lily's help, she's turned a spare bathroom into a makeshift lab, but it's nothing compared to the spacious and well-equipped lab she had in our old house.

"Did you put this letter in my office?" I ask her.

"Yeah. I think you have an admirer."

I frown. "Why would you say that?"

"Because it came with chocolates." She points at an open box of truffles on the table. "I didn't think you'd appreciate them, so I decided to give them a try. To test for poison, obviously."

I roll my eyes. "Obviously."

That must be the hint. Is there a chocolate factory in Attenburgh?

I pick up the box. It's black cardboard. One of the edges is dented, but that may have been Bethany's doing. There's no brand name or even a ribbon; just the box. Inside are ten compartments, although three of them are now empty. Glutton. The remaining seven chocolates are perfectly symmetrical balls, two dark, three white, the others light brown. I'm one for white chocolate, personally, but I resist from eating them. They might be clues that I need to solve this strange riddle.

"The chocolates you ate, what did they taste like?"

Bethany looks at me in confusion. "Like chocolate? Sweet. Delicious."

"Anything inside?"

"No. Actually, I was a little disappointed by that. I'd hoped for liquid chocolate, or maybe some alcohol, or even just a hazelnut, but it's just air."

That gives me hope. I lift one chocolate after another, gently shaking them. The brown ones all sound hollow, but one of the white balls is heavier than the others. I break it open – using my fingers rather than my teeth – and smile when a tiny plastic key becomes visible inside. It's no bigger than my thumbnail, but there's no doubt that it's a key. A folded piece of paper is underneath it.

I discard the chocolate and it's immediately snatched up by Bethany, who pops it in her mouth.

"You didn't need that anymore, did you?" she snickers. "Yummy."

I ignore her and unfold the paper. Five symbols are drawn on it in rough strokes. They seem familiar, but I can't remember where I've seen such signs before. I show it to Bethany.

"Any idea what this could mean?"

She shakes her head, still munching on chocolate. "No, but ask Benjamin. I know he learned all sorts of secret languages when he was working as a thief. They have lots of symbols to let each other know where the good hauls are, or when to stay away if too many guards are around."

"Thanks. Is he over in your building?"

"In our shack, you mean. And yes."

"Hey, it's a perfectly nice outbuilding. A secondary house. Not a shack."

She scoffs. "Easy for you to say, you live in the pretty big house. You don't have to listen to Benjamin's snoring."

She doesn't seem to be genuinely unhappy though. This is just Bethany's usual complaining. I hope. I don't want any discontent among my team. When I saw this property, I thought it was perfect. Enough space for all eight of us, plus work areas. I try to keep work and pleasure separate. It's easier here since I don't work every day, all day. Instead of fighting evil people, I'm fighting boredom.

I leave her to it – not expecting to ever see those chocolates again – and walk over to the other building. A paved garden connects the two, surrounded by high brick walls giving us privacy from neighbours. The house to our right is uninhabited and the cats have made it their own. To our left lives an old woman who's half-blind and all-deaf. She smiles at me whenever I see her and I smile back, pretending to be the perfect neighbour. If only she knew what's going on next door. We don't have any bodies here right now, but I bet it won't be too long until we've got yet another head in the fridge or some random limbs in the lab.

I hear Benjamin's snoring before I even enter the house. Lucky boy. I wish I was still asleep. Well, if I have to be awake, then he should be, too. Life isn't fair.

Two kittens lie in the short hallway leading to one large bedroom and to a narrow staircase. One of them completely ignores me and continues licking his paws, while the other, a stark white cat with grey ears, inclines his head in greeting. He's one of the older kittens, judging from his size.

"Want to wake Benjamin?" I ask him with a devilish grin.

I swear the kitten smiles back. He gets up and arches his back, then joins me as I climb the stairs to the first floor. Benjamin chose the smallest room for some reason. Not that I care. Bethany, Lily and he can do with their little house whatever they want. It's their realm.

The kitten meows when I open Benjamin's door. He runs in and I wait, a smile on my lips. Two seconds later, a scream lets me know that Benjamin is now awake. I stroll in, all innocence.

"Morning. Did the little kitten wake you?"

The cat in question is standing on Benjamin's face, his paws narrowly missing the young man's eyes.

"Don't pretend it was Muffin's idea," Benjamin growls. "He's usually very well-behaved."

The kitten looks at me as if he's just been insulted.

"I know, he's wrong," I tell Muffin. "You're most certainly not well-behaved."

He sends me his assent, before jumping off Benjamin and curling up at the end of the bed.

Benjamin glares at me. "What do you want? I was having such a lovely dream."

"It's late. The early cat catches the mouse."

"You don't like mornings either. Don't pretend you're up because you want to be. Have you had your appointment yet?"

I freeze. Oops. That.

"Not yet," I hedge. I check my watch. Damn, I'm late. That's not a good first impression.

I shove the piece of paper at Benjamin. "Do you recognise these symbols?"

He blinks, tiredness softening his features. "Yes, of course. You don't?"

I roll my eyes. "Would I be here otherwise? Can you write down the meaning for me? I need to go now, so just put it on my desk."

I turn, angry at myself for forgetting my meeting. I should have gone there straight after breakfast rather than going to my office. I guess I'm still getting used to my new life here. I used to have a routine. Now, I'm making it up as I go along.

"Run, kitty, run," Benjamin calls after me as I leave the house. I flip him off, even though he can't see it. It's satisfying nonetheless.

CHAPTER THREE

Attenburgh's town hall is an imposing building that towers over all the neighbouring houses. A market has been built around it, although only half the stalls are occupied today. I walk straight through them and up the marble stairs leading to the town hall's double doors. They're wide open, but I'm the only one going in. No guards to be seen anywhere. That surprises me. Attenburgh is a rich town, as can be seen from how this town hall has been built: fancy marble, expensive woods, jewels embedded in the doors. If I were in charge, I'd make sure nobody gets tempted by all that wealth. I can almost smell the riches in the town hall's vaults. It's a pity I'm not a common thief. Breaking in here could be fun, especially if the security is as lax as it seems.

A half-moon reception desk takes in most of the entrance hall. Two women stand behind it, both wearing elegant black costumes. A few people mill around the edges of the room, probably waiting for appointments.

"How can I help you?" one of the women asks me.

Her hair is an unnatural white-blonde; a colour that would only look natural if she were thirty years older.

"I've got a meeting with Lady Lara."

I don't mention that I'm half an hour late by now.

"Name?"

"Feln. Katriona Feln."

I'd pondered using a fake name, but in the end, it doesn't matter. I'm sure some members of the Pack know the name I chose for myself, and if they do, then they may have passed it on to the Fangs. Not that there's much left of the Pack. We burned their labs and most of their headquarters. When we left, their leaders were in hiding, abandoning the young shifters they'd enslaved. Luckily, we hadn't needed to deal with that ourselves. Mr Moon, Lennox's mentor, volunteered to look after them. I hope he's giving them the choice to stay or leave and try to survive on their own, but to be honest, I didn't want to push my luck, so I never asked him outright.

"You're late," the woman says with a disapproving frown.

As if I don't know. I don't apologise. It's not this receptionist who I've got a meeting with. She doesn't matter.

"Take the lift to the fourth floor and take a seat in the waiting area. I will see if Lady Lara can still meet you, or if she is now otherwise engaged."

I nod and turn to the elevator at the other end of the room. I hate lifts. They're metal boxes doomed to fail, taking their insides with them into the abyss. No, I'll take the stairs. Luckily, the door to the stairwell is clearly marked next to the elevators. I take two steps at a time, glad I'm not out of breath by the time I reach the fourth floor. I've not trained or even run as much since we moved here as I usually do.

A woman waits for me when I step out of the stairwell. Her white jumpsuit is a sharp contrast to her shimmering ebony skin. It's as if she accidentally sprayed glitter all over herself. Is that the latest fashion? Or is that natural? Her black hair is twisted into a sleek bun, which makes her look older than she probably is. Mid to late thirties, I'd guess. She's pretty, but not pretty enough to be a siren. Thank goodness. I'd hoped that she'd be human, and therefore less dangerous.

"Miss Feln?"

Her voice is surprisingly deep, but melodious.

I incline my head, remembering I need to be polite. "Lady Lara?"

"Indeed. You're late."

"Apologies, something came up."

"No matter. It gave me the chance to read a little. I barely have time for that nowadays." She smiles at me. "When I took this job, I didn't realise how much it would eat up my personal life. But let's take this to a more private space."

She leads me to a spacious office. The walls are clad in dark wood, but the furniture is all white and beige, making it less gloomy than it could have been. A tray with tea and biscuits awaits us on a small side table next to two leather armchairs. She beckons for me to sit down and I gladly do, sinking into the soft chair. I need one of those for my home. We've got two sofas, but they came with the house and are both threadbare and uncomfortable.

She takes a seat opposite me and pours us some tea. She hands me my cup with a smile, before leaning back in her chair, studying me intently.

"So, Miss Feln, you've applied for the position and I quite enjoyed your application. A lot less…blah than most of the others. I like people who're direct and who don't embellish their achievements. Of course, you've got a lot fewer qualifications than some of the other applicants, but I wanted to meet you nonetheless."

A lot fewer qualifications. I smirk. None, actually. It's not like the Pack gave me an education that went beyond learning how to kill, steal and torture. With a bit of poisoning and manipulation thrown in.

"How did you come across the job advert?" she continues.

"An acquaintance passed it on to me. I've only recently moved to this town and have been looking for a valuable use of my time. This seemed like the ideal thing to do."

Lady Lara quirks an eyebrow. "I'm glad you think this would be a *valuable* use of your time. Making sure I don't get killed would be *valuable* for me as well."

"Why are you concerned for your safety?" I ask. "The ad didn't say."

She laughs. "Of course it didn't. It's not like I want to tell my enemies that they've got to me. But after two assassination attempts in the past three weeks, I've decided it's time to stop tempting fate. I'm tired of having to constantly look over my shoulder. I need someone to do it for me."

"How did they try to kill you?"

"Poisoned gin – an anonymous present – and a knife at my throat. Luckily, the second assassin was badly trained and my self-defence skills were sufficient. But as I said, I don't expect to get away with my life a third time. That's where you come in."

I nod. "As I said in my application, I can assist you with both protection, and prevention of further attacks. If you know who's sending the assassins, it would be my pleasure to make sure they don't do it again."

"That won't be necessary. Not yet, anyway. As I said, I

don't want them to know that I'm worried. I'll continue my life and work as before, but I'll sleep safer knowing that there's someone watching out for new threats. You said you have experience in dealing with assassins?"

"Yes, I do."

Dealing as in working *with* them. Or making sure to reach the mark faster than them. But she doesn't have to know that. To be fair, I should be excellent at preventing assassins from hurting Lady Lara. I know how they think, how they operate. All I'd have to do is imagine how I would kill her, and then act accordingly.

"That's good. Very good. I much prefer real-world experience over certificates and degrees."

"There are degrees in fighting assassins?" I interrupt.

She laughs again. "No, but there are in psychology. Most of the applicants have some sort of background in profiling. Not you, though, and that's what made you stand out." She clears her throat. "Now, since I wasn't able to put much detail into the ad, here's what the job would entail. First, I need this room to be as secure as possible. I want to make sure nobody's spying on me. Then I need you to advise me on security. The previous mayor was exceptionally lax with guarding this building, but that's going to change from now on. I don't want anyone in this town hall who doesn't belong here. Once that's been sorted, I will occasionally need an escort when I'm at events or meetings. One not dressed like a bodyguard, but as a fellow guest, or as my assistant. It's custom not to bring guards to such events, but with the current situation, I cannot allow myself to go there alone."

I nod, making sure to hide how keen I am to get this job. This could open doors, offer new business opportunities, maybe even help me find my sister. Being close to the mayor is the best thing that could happen to me. Now I just need her to give me the job.

"If you don't mind me asking, why do people want to kill you so badly?" I ask. "As I said, I'm new to Attenburgh and I'm not yet familiar with the local politics."

She presses her lips together in a hard line, her previous humour gone in a flash. "Attenburgh has always been an extremely conservative place. Extravagant, gaudy, in-your-face, yes, but behind the scenes, the town was ruled by old men who clung to power. I'm the first female mayor ever. I embody the change that many are frightened of. I don't come from one of the powerful families. I don't have the money other politicians have. But I do have the support of the people and of most of the town council. That's how I got this position. And I intend to hold it."

Her eyes glint with conviction. "This town needs me. We've been divided by class for too long. The upper classes live in squalor while the ordinary people can barely make ends meet. That needs to change and I'll be the one to start the process of transforming Attenburgh."

I feel like I should applaud, but I simply nod and smile. "I can understand that not everybody likes that."

"Understatement of the century. It's a miracle that I've made it this far. I may be the mayor now, but I'm not arrogant enough to think that my enemies will just let me be. It's vital for me to find new supporters, powerful ones, which brings me back to the gatherings I have to attend. I admit, a lot of them are boring and tiresome, but sadly, they're necessary." She smirks. "Even though I'd rather stay here and deal with the important things. Like making sure everyone in this town has enough to eat. The salmon canapes seem to get stuck in my throat when I think of that. But sometimes, you have to befriend the devil to conquer hell."

Lady Lara sips her tea and I've realised I've not touched my own one yet. Our conversation has captured me enough to forget about my tea. That doesn't happen often. She really is an interesting woman. When I applied for this job, I thought the mayor would be a stuck-up old woman, stuffy with age and tradition. Instead, she's modern, progressive and in her thirties. I could come to like her. But I don't have the job yet. This is just an interview, even if it's a casual one.

"Do take a biscuit," she offers.

I'm not hungry, but I take one just to be polite. Out of habit, I give it a quick sniff – and freeze. The scent, like copper mixed with apple, is unmistakable.

"Don't touch them," I say sharply and throw my biscuit back on the plate. "They're poisoned."

Lady Lara shoots me a wicked grin. "They are indeed. Well done. Two applicants didn't realise."

I shudder. I was given this poison back in the Pack, when our teachers insisted that we needed to know what the non-lethal poisons felt like. I'd spent four days in bed, retching my guts out while fighting the most horrific hallucinations.

"Did you give them the antidote?"

"No. I assumed that if they were any good, they'd have their own supply. And if not…well, it'll teach them not to apply to jobs they're not suited for."

My respect for her grows. There's more to this woman than I first thought. She's wasted as a politician. I'd employ her in a heartbeat. With a bit of training, she could be magnificent.

"Are there any other tests?" I ask drily.

Her grin widens. "Who knows. Telling you would be boring. But since you passed this one, we can now talk about details. Like your pay."

I return her smile. "That's a very nice topic."

"Isn't it just. The figure in the ad was just a general idea. I would pay you that amount in your first month, and then, once I see what you're worth, I could easily increase, if not double it."

Inside, I'm laughing maniacally, but on the outside, I stay cool and collected. "Sounds good. I mentioned in my application that I have employees who all have their own unique skills. One of them, for example, is excellent with poisons, both creating and neutralising them. Since someone's tried to poison you once already, I'd suggest she supplies you with an assortment of antidotes, plus she can advise you on any measures you might want to take with your kitchen staff. She's not cheap, but she's the best."

"Naturally. Who else do you have in your team?"

"A repossession expert, two excellent fighters who could take my place if necessary, or join me at bigger events where one pair of eyes isn't enough. I'm also in the process of embedding one of my people in the higher layers of society, so if she uncovers information pertaining to you and your position, I'd of course pass that on."

"For a price."

I smirk. "Naturally. I can't go into detail, but I also have a network of spies across town. If you'd ever get into trouble while with me, they can help us make a quick exit and take the best shortcuts back to safety."

"Sounds like you've got it all figured out. Is this what you did where you lived before?"

I suppress a snort. If only she knew.

"Something similar."

She accepts my answer without asking me to go into detail. Good. I assume she's figured out by now that I'm not exactly used to being on her side of the law.

Lady Lara puts her cup down and gets up, extending a hand.

"When can you start?"

CHAPTER FOUR

When I get home, my family has gathered in the living room. Gryphon and Ryker are lounging on one sofa, while Caitlin is on the other. Lennox still hasn't returned from his wolf run. I'll give him until tomorrow before I go on the search for him. Or send the cats. That will be easier.

"How did it go?" Gryphon asks and moves over to make space for me.

I sit between the two guys and immediately, they both put a hand on my knees. Urgh. As nice as the gesture is, it makes me feel beleaguered and trapped. For now, I'll endure it, but if they go any further, I'll have to tell them off.

"Rather well. I got the job, and it looks like there'll be opportunities for most of us to get involved."

"Even me?" Caitlin asks.

I cringe. I don't quite know what to do with my sister. I think she's stable now, as long as she takes her potions, but am I ready to let her out into the world without supervision? Not yet. Caitlin is unpredictable, not just because of her past, but because she's my sister. All of us are strong-willed and independent. To be honest, I was surprised that Caitlin decided to come with us rather than set off on her own. Of course it's nice to have my sister around, to have the chance to get to know her further, but at the same time, I feel guilty for her having to stay inside.

"We'll see," I hedge, annoyed at myself when her smile drops. "For now, it's going to be just me, plus Bethany to supply Lady Lara with some antidotes in case she gets poisoned again."

"Someone tried to poison the mayor?" Gryphon asks sharply. "Is she a siren?"

"Yes and no. But she tried to poison me too." I smirk. "I kind of like her. She's tougher than she looks."

"She'd have to be to rise this high in a society dominated by sirens. How did she even do it?"

I shrug. "I'm sure I'm going to find out in time. She said that she has the support of the people and most of the town council. It seems to be enough to keep her in power, for now. Although there have been two assassination attempts on her, which is why she was looking for a bodyguard. Turns out, the role is going to be much broader than that."

I reach over and snatch a half-empty bag of crisps from Ryker. He's not eating them, so they're fair game.

"How broad?" the cat shifter asks.

"Securing her office, searching the kitchens and stores for poison, vetting her staff, employing more guards for the town hall, and a whole lot more. I also have an appointment with Lady Lara's tailor to get some outfits."

"Dresses?" Gryphon asks. "Please tell me it's dresses."

I elbow him in the ribs. "Unfortunately. If I accompany her to some high society events, I need to blend in. She doesn't want me to look like a bodyguard, but like a friend or assistant." I shudder. "Luckily, the pay is enough for me to squeeze into a dress."

Caitlin laughs. "I can't wait to see that. Especially the squeezing part. Have you seen how tiny the waists of some of the women here are? Good luck with that."

I shoot her a glare. "How do you even know that?"

She has the decency to look a little guilty. "You didn't think I'd stay cooped up here all day, did you. But don't worry, I've been careful. I've just gone to the market a couple of times to explore the area."

"I always had some of my cats following her," Ryker adds good-naturedly.

"You knew about this?" I groan. "Why is nobody ever doing what I say?"

Ryker laughs. "Because none of us are good at following rules. You should know that by now."

Urgh. He's right. I would have done the same had I been in Caitlin's shoes. That reminds me. I'll need to get shoes for my new job. I refuse to get anything with heels – as much as a sharp heel can be helpful in a fight, I do need to be able to run – but I'll concede to fancy flat shoes. I'll miss my leather boots with every step, but it's the price I'll have to pay for getting this job. I hope it'll be worth it.

"When do you start?" Gryphon asks.

"Tomorrow. Well, tomorrow is just for checking out the town hall's security and making plans on how to improve it. Lady Lara hasn't told me when she has any events planned that I need to accompany her to."

"Oh!" Caitlin exclaims and we all look at her.

"Yes?"

She pulls something from her pocket and reaches over the table to hand it to me.

"Almost forgot this. Benjamin asked me to give it to

you. He's gone for the rest of the day, so he wanted to make sure that you see it."

"Where is he?"

"Something to do with this. He didn't explain it to me."

I frown and unfold the piece of paper. It's a copy of the five symbols I found in the chocolate, with lots of scribbled notes all around. Benjamin's writing is tiny and not exactly legible. I sigh. This will take a while to decipher.

"What's this all about?" Ryker asks.

I give him a quick rundown of the mysterious letter and the chocolate riddle.

He chuckles when I've finished. "Now that sounds like a fun mission. Business opportunity of a lifetime. If you want, I can take over. Since you'll be busy with your new job."

I growl softly. "You wish. Although I'll allow you to help."

Ryker snickers. "How generous. Gryph, you in?"

"Obviously," the siren drawls. "It's not like I've got anything better to do."

And just like that, it's become a team effort. Maybe that's for the best. Ryker is right, I'll be busy looking after Lady Lara.

Gryphon snatches the paper from my hand and studies it. I growl again but let him be. Maybe he has better luck at deciphering Benjamin's awful handwriting.

"Interesting," he mutters. "Each symbol stands for a location. Benjamin has figured out four of them, but wasn't sure about the fifth. I assume that's what he's doing just now, finding out where the fifth is."

"Locations?" Gryphon asks. "Explain."

"It looks like the symbols are a riddle in themselves. Benjamin has scribbled the meaning beside the symbols, and then the solution next to that. The first one meant water, castle, flag. He's interpreted that as the big stone bridge over the river, the one with the walls that look like they belong to a castle. In the middle of the bridge is a tower with a flag on top. I assume that's where the next clue is."

I rack my brain for the bridge he's talking about. Attenburgh is built on both sides of a river, with dozens of bridges connecting the two halves. When I first moved here, I assumed that the posh people would live on one side and the poor citizens on the other, but surprisingly, it's all mixed. Our house is on the North side, although we're quite far from the river, being at the very edges of town.

I've definitely walked over that bridge, but I can't say that I noticed a flag.

"Then there's a house by the market with a cockerel, an underwater location at the deepest point of the river, and a basement that was once used to store wine. The fifth one has lots of question marks. Let's see what Benjamin says when he gets back."

"We could take one location each," Caitlin suggests with a wicked grin.

I know exactly what she's trying to do. Get out of the house without supervision.

I sigh. "How about you take Bethany or Lily with you? I don't need Beth until tomorrow and it might do her good to get some fresh air. She's spent way too long in her new lab."

"Bathroom," Gryphon chuckles. "As she points out every time we talk."

"Okay," Caitlin concedes. "But if they're busy or don't want to go, then I'll do it on my own. I'm not a child."

No, she's not. She's been through more than most adults have, just like all of us sisters. But I'm the oldest and

I feel like it's my job to protect my younger siblings. I never had a family before and I'm not going to let anyone take them from me.

"I'll take the cockerel," Ryker says, licking his lips. "I'm hungry."

Gryphon laughs. "You do know it's likely just a carving or wall painting?"

Ryker shrugs. "A cat can hope."

"Since none of you felines will want to do the underwater location, I'll take that one," Gryphon volunteers to my delight. I'd already planned to make him do it, but it's nice that he thinks it was his idea.

"That leaves the bridge and the basement," I summarise. "Caitlin, which one do you want to do?"

"The bridge. I'm not a fan of basements." She smiles bravely.

"Alright. I don't know what we're looking for, so keep your eyes open for anything that looks out of place. More strange symbols, hidden messages, graffiti and so on."

It all feels a bit like a wild goose chase, but since we don't have anything better to do, why not.

I take one more look at what Benjamin has scribbled before getting up from the sofa.

"We've got a couple of hours of daylight left. If you want to check out your locations today, I suggest you leave now."

"I'll make some snacks to take with us," Caitlin volunteers.

Gryphon laughs. "It's not like we're going on an expedition. One quick look at the locations and we'll be back home."

Caitlin's smile wavers, so I intervene, unwilling to see my sister unhappy.

"Go, make us something for the road. I'm hungry anyway, since nobody has bothered to cook today."

I shoot a glare at the guys and they're good enough to look guilty. We've not quite figured out a food rota yet. With all of us home at different times, it's hard to make sure everyone gets at least one hot meal a day. Sure, Bethany and Benjamin don't mind; they live off snacks and junk food, but the rest of us need proper food to make sure we stay healthy. Being an assassin takes a surprising amount of vitamins. And catnip, obviously. That's my favourite vegetable.

While Caitlin disappears into the kitchen, I head up to my office to make sure no more mysterious letters have arrived. Nothing. I give the desk a gentle pat - a promise that I will sit down and go through all the paperwork eventually - and go to my bedroom to get changed. I'm wearing my prettiest outfit and it's not exactly suitable for exploring dark and dirty basements. I change into my almost-assassin clothes; black and durable, but not the jumpsuit I prefer. That one would draw attention during the day. It's perfect to blend into the night, but I don't want to wait until evening.

It's time to solve a mystery...and hopefully get rich in the process.

CHAPTER FIVE

Benjamin's directions are vague, but I make it into the trading district with only a few wrong turns. I've only been here once before; there's not much to see or do. Workshops and small shops line the streets, with old warehouses lined up behind them. Craftsmen of all trades work here, creating their goods in the privacy of their workshops, before selling them at the market or shipping them off to other towns.

The roads aren't too busy and I make quick progress even without taking to the roofs.

Benjamin narrowed the basement's location down to Tanner's Street. It takes me a while to find it. A map would have been nice, but I never even thought of that. I'm not used to being in places I don't know. Back home, I would have laughed in the face of whoever suggested I'd need a map. Oh well, soon I'll know Attenburgh just as well.

Tanner's Street is right across Tanner's Alley and around the corner from Tanner's Court. Damn. Was Benjamin certain about it being called Street? If I'm unlucky, I'll have to search the basements in all three. That could take forever.

The only other clue is that the cellar was once used to store wine. Maybe I'll find an old winery, although that would be a little too easy.

I sigh. If I want to save time, I'll actually have to talk to people. To humans. I usually avoid that when I can. I've been too sociable today already, spending over an hour with Lady Lara. But it's the best option I have.

Urgh.

I approach an old lady sitting on a wooden bench outside a shop. She's knitting, but her eyes are closed as she enjoys the sun. Almost like a cat. I'm tempted to shift and do the same, just lie here and soak up the sun's warmth, but that would raise more than a few eyebrows. Pitchforks and knives too.

"Excuse me," I ask as nicely as I can. "Do you know if there was ever a winery in this area? Or maybe a wine store?"

She doesn't open her eyes, but a smile moves over her wrinkled face.

"You're the second person who's asked me this today, my dear. Are you in the wine business?"

"No, it's more of a personal interest."

"Well, then I'm afraid to disappoint you. I've lived here for eighty years and there's never been anything to do with wine here. The folk here drink beer and whisky rather than wine." She chuckles. "If you want wine, you'll have to go to other parts of town. The only thing people here use grapes for is vinegar."

Vinegar. Made from grapes. Could it be?

I wish I could read the symbols myself. I have no idea how accurate they are. Maybe it didn't even say wine but grapes, and Benjamin assumed that it would be wine that's made from them. Either way, this is the only lead I have.

"Could you tell me where they may have stored barrels of vinegar?" I ask the woman. "Maybe a cellar somewhere?"

"I think there was one in Tanner's Court," she replies thoughtfully. "If you walk down the street from here, you'll pass a ruined building to your right. Two or three houses from there was the old distillery. I don't know how much is left of it though."

"I'll take a look. Thank you."

I turn to leave, but then remember something.

"The other person who asked about this. What did they look like?"

The old woman chuckles. "Oh dear, how would I know?"

She opens her eyes for the first time, revealing milky pupils. She's blind.

"Sorry," I mutter.

"It was a man, I can tell you that much. And he had a lisp. Definitely a local. But that's all I can tell you."

"Thank you, you've been a great help."

Her smile widens. "I'm glad I can still be helpful occasionally. Before you go, I think I can smell cats. Is there one nearby? I so love petting cats."

Oops. It must be me she's smelling. Still, that's one wish I can easily fulfil. I whistle a high-pitched sound, inaudible to the human ear, but strong enough to alert any cat in the vicinity.

It only takes a few seconds for a midnight black cat to appear. He's one of Ryker's. I don't know his name, but I recognise him by his three white paws.

He looks at me curiously. I nod towards the old woman

and send him a mental message. He purrs and jumps on the bench, snuggling against her thigh.

"Oh, you found the cat!" she exclaims and reaches out to stroke his head. He purrs even more and closes his eyes in delight at both the attention and the sun.

Lucky him.

I leave them to it and walk down Tanner's Court, passing the ruined house just like the old woman described. The street is quiet, almost too much so. Most of the buildings here are in disrepair and I doubt many of them are still used. The perfect place for shady activities.

It's easy to find the house in question; the worn-out sign with the grapes kind of gives it away. Curiously, the grape on the sign is surrounded by three bones that form a triangle. Vinegar strong enough to kill? Or did they use bones as their secret ingredient? Who knows.

I extend my senses. The building is abandoned and nobody has been here in days. The other guy looking for this place must not have found it. Maybe the old woman didn't tell him about the vinegar distillery. Or he didn't listen. Most men don't.

Making sure that nobody is watching, I try the door. It's unlocked. I'm either really lucky or someone is making this easy. Too easy.

With all my senses on full alert, I enter the building. Dust coats the floor. A few footprints are still visible, but they were made months ago, judging from how the dust has almost hidden them. The room is mostly empty, with the exception of a few bits of wooden furniture stacked in one corner. As if someone had planned to move them to a new place and then forgot.

On the opposite end of the room are two doors. One's open and leads to some stairs, while the other one is closed.

I walk over to that one, treading as lightly as I can. Still, there's no way to avoid leaving footprints in the dust.

The door is locked, but it's no match for my trusted lockpicks. It opens with a groan; I doubt the hinges have been oiled in the past twenty years. Just like I'd hoped, a narrow staircase leads down into a basement. Bingo.

The air in the cellar is stuffy, as if the oxygen has been sucked out. The acrid smell of vinegar tickles my nose and burns my throat. Damn those super-sensitive senses. I'd prefer to be human sometimes, walking through life with no idea how intense the world can be.

Just like the room above, the basement is mostly empty. Two shelves line the walls to both sides of me; so old that I wouldn't risk putting anything heavy on them. A tiny window above one of the shelves lets in a bit of light, enough to see.

A single barrel sits in the centre of the room. Weird. Again, a sense of foreboding grips me. This is too easy. There has to be a trap. Or something else that would make it harder and more dangerous.

If this is it, then I'm very disappointed in Attenburgh's underworld.

I circle the barrel, making sure there are no tripwires or other obstacles. Nothing. How boring. I've not encountered a decent lethal trap in ages. They used to send us through obstacle courses back in the Pack, and quite a few of us got seriously injured or even died. I almost lost a finger once. That training taught me a lot, no matter how much I hate the Pack.

Once I'm almost sure that there are no traps, I throw a knife at the lid of the barrel. The lid collapses, breaking into several pieces of wood. I don't think that was intentional; simply a side-effect of age. Cautiously, I approach the barrel and peek inside. An envelope sits at the very bottom, it's white paper a stark contrast to its dirty surroundings. I reach out and take it.

So boring. Why are there no traps when I want them?

Out of habit, I sniff the envelope - and grin. Finally. The Attenburghers - is that what the people of this city call themselves? - really like poison.

If I'm not completely mistaken, then this is Lord's Kiss, a lethal poison that the aristocracy prefer. It's quick, painless and hard to spot when it's hidden in food or drink. Inside an envelope though, the characteristic smell of mouldy roses is easy to detect.

I put the envelope into a sealed bag to make sure it doesn't contaminate anything I've got stashed in my pockets. It's time to go back home and look at what I found - after I've removed the poison. I have no intention of dying today.

I SEEM TO BE THE FIRST ONE BACK, SO I HEAD STRAIGHT TO Bethany's bathroom lab and start preparing the envelope. Lord's Kiss is only activated when it comes in contact with water, which is why it works best in drinks. However, if even a few grains of it entered my mouth and mixed with my spittle, I'd probably fall ill for a few days.

I slow down my breathing and keep my lips pressed together while I empty the envelope of all poison. Instead of discarding it, I store it in a small box. I'd be foolish to throw away such an expensive substance. I might have use for it in the future, and if I don't, then it's likely that one of the other M.E.O.W. employees will.

I clean the envelope and the letter inside with a vinegar

solution - how very appropriate - until I'm sure that no poison remains.

Finally, I get to read the mysterious letter. This has taken a long time just to find an envelope. I really hope it's worth it.

CHAPTER SIX

Benjamin is in the living room, looking broody. Two kittens sit on either side of him - well, one of them is lying on her back, snoring softly.

"Didn't find what you were looking for?" I ask.

He doesn't look up, but continues to stare at the book in his hands. It's a small, leather-bound volume that I'm pretty sure I've not seen before. He must have found or bought it.

"What's the book?"

Still no reply.

I sigh. "Did the kittens eat your tongue?"

He finally looks up and glares at me. He opens his mouth.

Yuck. I suck in a breath. The insides of his mouth are bright green and his tongue is swollen to twice its normal size. No wonder he's not talking.

"What the fuck happened to you?"

He points at the book.

"A trap?"

He nods.

"Ouch. Does it hurt?"

To my relief, he shakes his head. I'm not sure I've ever heard of a poison with this effect. Maybe Bethany knows. Let's hope she returns soon. Benjamin doesn't seem to have any other symptoms, but I don't want to risk him becoming seriously ill. Or cursed to have a massive green tongue for the rest of his life.

"I assume you found that book in the location the symbol hinted at?" I ask.

Benjamin nods and hands it to me. The book is heavier than it looks. The pages are thick, which also means that there aren't a lot of them. A short read - if only the pages weren't blank.

I sigh. "Why can't they make things easy just once? Have you tried goose essence yet?"

He shakes his head and points at his mouth.

"Ah yes, you had other things to worry about. Let me go and grab some from the lab. If this is invisible ink, then we'll know soon."

There are several ways to make written words invisible, but one of the most common methods can be made visible with goose essence. As far as I know, it's got nothing to do with geese. No idea where they got that name from, but I don't really care. As long as it works, it could be called Cat's Bloody Ovaries. Or maybe not.

When I return to the living room with a bottle of goose essence, Benjamin has found a hand mirror and is pulling faces, looking at his swollen tongue from all angles.

"Hhhhrmph."

"Sorry, I don't understand you."

He rolls his eyes.

"Offffff hffffff."

"Nope, still not getting it. It's probably best if you don't talk. Both for your health and your dignity."

He glares at me, but shuts his mouth.

"Kittens, can you go and find Bethany? Gryphon, too, just in case. Just meow at them for a while and they'll get the message."

They look at me in annoyance, but dutifully jump off the sofa and run out of the room. Ryker's got them trained well. They know that they've got a safe home here, with as much food as they need, as long as they work for it. Compared to what I had to do while growing up, they're practically living in a five-star hotel. Catnip included.

I put Benjamin's book on the low table in front of us and use a brush to carefully transfer some goose essence onto the first page. It works almost immediately.

Blue ink appears on the previously blank page. It's a clean, beautiful handwriting; quite the opposite to the scribbles Benjamin left us earlier.

The only problem is that it's written in a different language.

"Any idea what this could mean?" I ask Benjamin.

He learns forward to look at the book, but shakes his head.

"Hhhhhhrrmppphh."

"Yeah, I got that from you shaking your head. Don't talk. You continue with putting goose essence on the other pages. Maybe they're not all in the same language. I'll look at the letter I found."

I'm certain I've removed all traces of poison, yet I still stop breathing when I unfold the letter, just in case. I already had a quick look at it in the lab, but only to see that there was something written on it. I'd wanted to draw out the suspense for a little longer.

Congratulations. You have found me. I am one of five puzzle pieces. Put me together with my friends and we will tell you where to go next. As a reward for getting this far, and not dying in the process, here's a token of our appreciation.

A six-digit code is drawn beneath the typed writing.

"Well, that's interesting," I mutter. "Seems we have two puzzle pieces now, even though I have no idea where the puzzle is. This is just a letter, right? Plus a number that we don't know what to use it for."

"Hhhhhmmmmrrrr."

Benjamin beckons me to give him the letter. I hand it over and he brushes some goose essence on it. Ah. Good thinking.

"Aaaahhhfffm!"

An image appears beneath the typed text. No, a map. Now that's handy.

"Well done." I snatch the letter back. "It's a map of Attenburgh. Not all of it, just the part south of the Atten river. And there are two locations marked. One of them is actually not very far from here."

I flick my ears to a sound in the distance before I realise that I'm human and can't do my panther ear flicking. Oh well. I flick them in a metaphorical way. It's Gryphon, accompanied by two cats.

"Gryphon's coming," I tell Benjamin. Poor human. He's cursed with bad senses. "He'll be able to look at your tongue. It's quite handy to have an almost-doctor in the family, right?"

Benjamin nods weakly. I may be mistaken, but I think his lips are starting to turn green too. Bad sign. Let's hope Bethany returns soon. I may know a lot about poisons, but she's a true expert. She has an instinctual way with them, sometimes knowing the recipe for an antidote without ever having read about it. I'd say she may have a herb witch in her ancestry, but there are no witches.

"We're in the living room!" I shout as soon as Gryphon enters the house.

He runs into the room, out of breath. "What's wrong? Are you hurt? The kitten was very insistent that I come immediately, so-"

I wordlessly point at Benjamin, who's opened his mouth to expose his green tongue.

"Ah," Gryphon sighs, his relief obvious that it's not me who needs his help. "That looks...interesting."

Benjamin glares at the siren.

"Some kind of poison," I explain. "The letter I found was covered in Lord's Kiss, but I'm not sure what substance Benjamin got in contact with. Bethany hasn't returned yet, but I've sent the cats to fetch her."

Gryphon nods and kneels in front of Benjamin, examining him closely.

"Say Ahhhh."

The thief shoots him a deathly glare, but opens his mouth and gurgles something that vaguely resembles Ahhhh."

"Kat, get me my med kit, please. I need some of my tools to deal with this."

Benjamin's eyes widen. He's probably picturing scalpels and injections, just like me. Poor thing.

I collect Gryphon's medical supplies from his room and stop by the kitchen to grab some snacks. I doubt Benjamin can eat in his current state, but I'm feeling peckish. I'll try not to make him too jealous.

When I return to the living room, I can't suppress a giggle at the sight of Benjamin spread out on the sofa and Gryphon straddling his hips, as if they're having some rather hot sex. Gryphon turns to me and rolls his eyes.

"It's not what you're thinking."

"I'm not thinking anything. But maybe heal Benjamin before you explore your gay tendencies."

He wiggles his eyebrows at me. "They're more than just tendencies."

"Oh? Tell me more."

He grins and turns back to poor Benjamin, who's still got his mouth open. I don't envy dentists. I bet they sometimes have to see some rather gruesome things.

"Scalpel," he says in his best doctor voice, causing Benjamin to shriek and buck up in fear.

Gryphon roars with laughter. "Alright, let's go with the scapula instead. And some gloves. I really don't want to touch that monster tongue."

"Hrrrrrmphhh."

I hand him his supplies, glad it's him who's doing it and not me. I'm not squeamish – I torture people for a living – but seeing Benjamin's green mouth is doing weird things to my stomach. I'm lucky that I recognised Lord's Kiss, otherwise I'd be in his position or worse.

Footsteps outside alert me to new arrivals. Bethany, Caitlin and Lily. It's a good excuse to step out of the room and brush my retinas, erasing what I've just seen. Not the tongue bit. The Gryphon-riding-Benjamin image. It's strangely arousing, at least if I imagine Benjamin to be someone else. Nothing involving Benjamin is arousing; he's just a scrawny boy.

"Hey honey, I'm home!" Lily shouts as soon as she steps through the front door. "Honeys. Is that the plural of honey? Maybe I should just say sweethearts."

I roll my eyes. She's in one of her succubus moods, characterised by her finding everyone cute and adorable. I hope she won't try and kiss me again.

"I met Bethany and Caitlin on the way," she chatters in hyper speed. "They were in a bit of a hurry, so I went along rather than visit one of my boyfriends for a little aperitif. You know, the one I told you about, the one with the massive thighs and the long-"

"Shut it," Bethany growls. "You're making me appreciate being single. Now what's the problem, Kat? Why did you call me back?"

"Benjamin had a bit of a poison accident. Gryphon's with him now, but I think you should take a look."

"The siren's trying to fix a poisoning? Hah, as if."

She stomps off towards the living room, followed by Caitlin, leaving Lily and me behind. We exchange a look and break into laughter.

"She's so adorable," Lily mutters with a half-moan. "I wonder if she-"

"No. No relationships between M.E.O.W. employees. You know the rule."

"Blah. Does that apply to Benjamin and Bethany as well? If you could sense the attraction between those two…"

Attraction? I sniff the air, but can't find any trace of arousal. Hopefully, it's just Lily messing with me. The two Bs…I can't imagine them being a couple. Benjamin is too young and Bethany way too unstable and selfish. She's a mess even on her good days. Her holding up a relationship would be a miracle. And I don't believe in those.

"Beth told me about the weird treasure hunt you've been on. Typical. As soon as I leave the house, you guys go on adventures. Did you find the treasure yet?"

I shake my head. "Only more puzzle pieces. We're still waiting for Ryker to return, then we can see what we found. If Bethany even had the chance to get to her location before the cats told her to come home."

"Oh yes, she did, she told me about it. Caitlin climbed

the tower on the bridge and people thought she was going to jump. Quite the commotion, apparently."

I cringe. That's the opposite of what I wanted. We're supposed to lay low, all of us, especially Caitlin. I should have told her to stay home.

"I know what you're thinking," Lily says and waves her index finger in front of my nose. "But you need to let her have some freedom. Having her cooped up inside the house will only make things worse. She needs to breathe and find herself. She's been given orders all her life; she probably has no idea who she really is. And she won't find the answers in this house."

"She won't find them either if she's arrested because they think she's suicidal," I snap. "Besides, she's my sister. It's my duty to protect her."

"There's a difference between protecting and smothering. Right now, you're leaning towards the latter."

I grimace. "That's because I'm an assassin. I'm good at smothering. To death."

Lily laughs. "Don't let her hear that."

"I heard it!" Caitlin shouts from the living room.

Damn, I forgot she has the same perfect senses I have. It's hard to have secrets when half the people in this house can hear everything that goes on in these walls.

Her words are followed by a terrified scream. Benjamin. Fuck.

I run to the living room, preparing myself for the worst, but I stop in my tracks as soon as I step through the door. Benjamin sits on the sofa, no longer green, and laughing hysterically at my expression.

"All healed," Bethany says with a proud grin. "That was easier than I thought."

I glare at Benjamin. People don't usually manage to

scare me. I've got too attached. I'm becoming way too human. That needs to change.

"What was it?" I ask Bethany, pointedly ignoring the thief.

"A mixture of several poisons. I washed his mouth with vinegar, then-"

"Wait, vinegar?" I interrupt. "That's a bit of a strange coincidence."

"Why?"

I explain the connection.

"Maybe the five puzzle pieces are connected," Bethany says thoughtfully. "Maybe they each offer a poison and the antidote. I shall look into that later. For now, I need to wash my hands. I don't want green spittle all over me."

No, I wouldn't want that either.

Gryphon follows her to clean up his equipment, which it seems he didn't actually need. Bethany did all the healing. As good as she is with poisoning people, I'm starting to think that she's even better with the opposite.

It seems we're all changing. I'm turning from a killer into a bodyguard. Bethany from a poisons master to a healer. If I'm not careful, we'll end up as a group of do-gooders protecting the innocent and running a hospital for the poor.

Yeah. No way.

CHAPTER SEVEN

By the time all of us are assembled in the living room, night has fallen. Lily has made us some sandwiches, which we've wolfed down in record speed. Pun intended. The only one still missing is Lennox. His absence leaves a strange empty feeling in my stomach. I can't quite place it.

Everyone's inspected the map I found and the book that Benjamin recovered. Sadly, none of the others recognises the language in there either. Gryphon has brought another letter, Ryker a small locket, and Caitlin a locked wooden box that resembles a tiny coffin, about as long as a pen.

Bethany has checked everything for poison, but we'll still have to be careful when opening the box and the locket.

We've spread out our finds on the table in our centre. Such a curious assortment of items. Whoever's organised this put a lot of effort into making sure that only those with certain abilities and knowledge could find out what this is all about. People without poison skills would be dead by now. Maybe they are. I wish I knew how many people this letter was sent to.

I realise they're all waiting for me to take charge. Or maybe they're just in post-food coma and don't want to engage their brains. Either way, I pick up the locket and study it closely. It's made from cheap metal and has no inscription or decoration that would give us a clue to its contents. It looks like it was once on a chain, but now it's only the locket. I put on my leather gloves and make sure nobody is sitting too close.

"Hold your breath," I order, before opening the locket. I almost expected some sort of poison inside – it would have fit the theme – but all the locket contains is a small plastic key, matching the one I found in the chocolate. Their teeth are slightly different, but I bet they'll both be needed at the same time to open a particular lock.

Benjamin takes the keys from me and studies them closely. "I can make copies of them, just in case. That way, if one of us comes across the lock they fit into, we don't have to return here."

"Good thinking. Maybe there's another key in the box."

I again make sure that everyone's holding their breath before carefully opening the wooden box. A thin vial is inside, protected by green velvet and containing a clear liquid. I hand it to Bethany, whose eyes are glowing with interest.

She unstoppers the vial and gives it a sniff, before starting to laugh.

"I think this is the antidote to whatever Benjamin was given. It contains vinegar with some additional substances. I'll take a closer look later in my lab, that might tell us more about its origins. But I doubt it's relevant to the puzzle. Just a way to make sure the adventurers don't all die."

Adventurers. I guess that's what we are, in a way. Detectives. Seekers.

That leaves the envelope Gryphon brought.

"Did you get wet?" Caitlin asks him. "Since you had the underwater location?"

Gryphon laughs. "No, luckily not. It was a tunnel beneath the river. Moist and damp, covered in rat droppings, but at least I didn't have to go swimming in the icy river."

Caitlin licks her lips. "Maybe I should have come. I love rats."

An awkward silence follows her words. With three simple words, she's managed to point out just how different she is. I assume that she didn't get enough food, just like the rest of us in the Pack. But at least we were allowed to roam the city when on assignments, which gave me the chance to steal some food at the market. She didn't have that opportunity. Instead, she ate rats.

A shiver runs down my back. If I hadn't already killed the Pack leaders, I'd do it again and again. With a lot more torture involved. I have done bad things, but I don't think I'm evil. They, however, were rotten and twisted inside. I was taught to kill for fun. They were born evil.

Gryphon clears his throat. "Kat, are you going to open that envelope? I didn't have the time; your kitten arrived just when I wanted to."

"I may have peeked inside while making sure there's no poison left," Bethany admits. "So don't get all overexcited. It's boring."

"Left?" I ask. "Does that mean that there was poison inside?"

She nods. "More Lord's Kiss, just like in your envelope.

A bit dull, if you ask me. It's as if they don't know any other poisons."

"Not everyone has their own lab."

"Bathlab," she corrects me. "And yes, I'm going to remind you of that until you build me a proper one."

I sigh. "You know that you won't get a lab until I know if we're going to stay here or not. So don't complain, it's not like we've not tried to make the best out of what we have."

She mutters something beneath her breath that I pointedly pretend not to hear. I'm too tired to start yet another argument with her. It's getting late and I have another meeting with Lady Lara tomorrow.

I take the envelope and pull out a folded piece of paper. The typed font is the same as on the letter I recovered. This one, however, doesn't make much sense. It's rows upon rows of letters and numbers that intermingle in a seemingly random manner. I don't see a pattern, but I'm not an expert in that either.

I hand the letter to Lily. "One for you. Maybe this could be the key to what's in the book?"

Her excitement is almost smellable. "I'll take a look, but it might take a while. Codebreaking isn't a fast process."

I yawn. "Take as long as you need. I'm going to bed; I have to get up early tomorrow. Bethany, want to accompany me to the town hall? You'll be responsible for making sure there are no poisons hidden anywhere in the kitchens, as well as putting some procedures in place to prevent anything harmful to be put into Lady Lara's food."

"How early?" she asks with a frown.

"Before either of us would usually get up. But the sooner we earn money from the mayor, we'll be able to buy more goodies for your lab."

Her eyes light up at that. "I could do with a new centrifuge. And maybe-"

"Just come with m tomorrow and we'll talk about it," I yawn. "Ryker, can you tell some of your cats to focus on the town hall and look for anything suspicious? Gryphon, do you want to be in charge of recruiting some new guards?"

Both men nod. They're so much easier to handle than Bethany.

"What about me?" Caitlin asks. "What can I do?"

She looks so desperate for something to do that I make a decision I'll likely regret.

"I'm putting you in charge of solving this puzzle. You can work with whoever can help or has the time, like Lily for deciphering the code, but I'm leaving it to you to figure it all out. Think you can do that?"

Caitlin nods eagerly. "I won't disappoint you."

"I never expected you would," I say gently. "But now let's go to bed. It's been a long day."

BOTH RYKER AND GRYPHON END UP IN MY BED. RYKER likes to sleep naked, while Gryphon is wearing silk pyjama pants. Posh bastard.

Surrounded by them, my tiredness wanes a little, especially when Gryphon slides a hand beneath my shirt. I prefer to sleep with an oversized t-shirt and panties. In case of emergencies, I don't want to run around naked – and in my line of work, emergencies happen frequently, even if it's just a well-paid hit than needs to be done immediately.

Still, the guys like that my large shirt gives them enough access. They shift closer until I'm sandwiched between them. Gryphon lifts up my shirt and cups my breast, gently massaging it just the way I like it, while Ryker's fingers end up between my legs after he's pulled down my panties.

I moan when he enters me while rubbing his thumb against my nub at the same time. He knows exactly how to play me like an instrument, creating moans like notes on a violin. Gryphon removes his hands from my breasts and I growl in protest, but then his lips close around my nipple and everything is fine again. He suckles, nibbles, suckles some more, until I'm raw with need. It's not enough.

I arch my back, basically shoving my breast into his mouth, while signalling Ryker that I need more than just his fingers. My siren laughs and starts massaging my other breast with one hand and stroking across my bottom lip with his other. I greedily suck on his fingers as if they're another part of his anatomy. I turn my head to one side to see if he's ready. Oh yes. He certainly is.

Ryker pushes a third finger into me. I push my pelvis towards him, needing him to reach down into the depths of my core. He fucks me with his fingers, while rubbing his thumb over my clit again and again. I'm hovering close to the edge, but it's not quite enough, not until Ryker kisses me between my legs and starts to lap up my wetness.

I come with a scream as his tongue flicks my clit, propelling me to new heights of pleasure. I'm flying, carried by my two mates, safe in their arms, away from all trouble and sorrow.

I'm so lost in the moment that I only realise someone else has entered the room when the bed groans under the extra weight.

"I see you started without me," Lennox whispers. "I hope you're not too tired to feel a wolf inside you."

CHAPTER EIGHT

I wake feeling surprisingly refreshed. Yes, I yawn several times, but that's more habit than anything else.

All three men are still sleeping. Gryphon and Ryker are still to either side of me, while Lennox is curled up at my feet. Silly doggo. His skin is radiant, almost glowing, as always after a full moon. He'll be full of energy for the next couple of days. I grin. I shall have to make sure to schedule in some extra bedroom time with him. He gets grumpy when he doesn't get to expend that energy…and besides, sex with a hyperactive werewolf is legendary. You've not had real sex until you've been with a randy wolf, or a seductive siren using his magic, or a cat shifter pumped full of catnip. Luckily, I have all three at my disposal.

I don't bother being quiet or careful when climbing out of the bed. If I have to get up, they have to, too. Being in a relationship means sharing, right? Including early mornings.

"Where are you off to?" Lennox asks with a loud yawn.

Ah. He doesn't know all that's happened yesterday.

"I'll tell you over breakfast. You've missed a lot."

He gives me his best puppy eyes.

"Alright then, if you don't want to have breakfast with me, the guys will fill you in. I have an appointment with the mayor and I was already late yesterday, I can't do that again."

"The mayor? You got the job?"

"Don't look so surprised. I was the best candidate. I survived her interview, poisoning attempt included."

His eyes widen. "Okay, I think I want to hear that story after all."

I give him a full rundown of yesterday's events while I make us some eggs on toast. They're very brown – I don't want to say burned – but they're just about edible. Lennox complains, as always, but if he doesn't like it, then he could have cooked. I shut up his moaning with a glare.

"If you want better food, get us a cook."

"Are you serious? You'd let a stranger in here to cook for us?"

"If you say it like that…no. Maybe we should pay for some cooking classes for Caitlin. She doesn't have much to do at the moment. Might as well make herself useful."

"You want to let your psychotic serial killer sister make our food?"

I poke him with my fork. "She's not psychotic. Her meds are working well."

He rolls his eyes. "I know. I was teasing you. And actually, I agree. It would give her some purpose."

"Then I'll leave it to you to find her a teacher. The job for the mayor is paying nicely, so we can afford it."

He nods. "On it. By the way, does the mayor know what you are?"

"I didn't tell her, but I doubt she'd be mayor of

Attenburgh without at least some knowledge of the supernatural. This city is full of sirens. I'm planning to lead the conversation in that direction today. Let's see how much she'll admit to knowing."

"Good idea. Want me to come with you?"

"I was planning to take Gryphon, but since he's not awake yet...How much do you know about securing a building?"

Lennox grins. "I helped Mr Moon come up with the security measures for his compound. I'm your wolf."

"Excellent. Then we just have to put on some pretty clothes, wake Bethany and we're ready to go." I grimace. "This isn't going to be pretty."

BETHANY PUTS UP A FIGHT UNTIL I REMIND HER THAT THIS job might pay for her future lab. And the new centrifuge she wants so desperately. Still, she complains the entire way to the town hall, which is a solid twenty minutes of whining.

By the time we get there, I'm ready to strangle her. I wish she'd been the one to have a massive green tongue. Bethany, unable to speak...what a wonderful image.

The receptionist waves us through and we take the stairs to the fourth floor. Accompanied by more of Bethany's grumbling, of course.

Just like yesterday, Lady Lara meets us by the staircase, smiling widely.

"You're on time," she says with a wink. "Well done."

I shrug. "So are you."

"Indeed. Who are your companions?"

I introduce Lennox and Bethany, calling him my Head of Security and her my Poisons Mistress. They both smirk at their new titles. Maybe I'm exaggerating a little, but first impressions count. I want Lady Lara to think that I'm up to the job and that my team is as good as I claimed in the interview.

"I have prepared a little test," Lady Lara announces with an innocent smile. "There are three traps hidden on this floor. Mr Lennox, if you can find and disarm them, you're hired. Ladies, come with me to my office, I have some poisons there to try."

She turns and confidently strides to her room. I exchange a look with the others.

"She's hardcore," Bethany whispers. "I like her."

Lennox sighs. "I better find those traps. See you later."

Bethany and I follow Lady Lara into the same office we met in yesterday. Instead of biscuits, three black bottles are lined up on the table.

Lady Lara waves her hand towards them. "One is deadly, one will injure, one is harmless. Drink the harmless one."

Bethany doesn't flinch. She keeps her poker face as she sits down and inspects the bottles.

"Take your time," Lady Lara says. "I have some things to discuss with Miss Feln."

"Kat, please. Miss Feln makes me feel ancient."

"Then you may call me Lara. Lady Lara makes me feel way too important." She smirks. "Of course I am, but I don't want to become too arrogant."

We move to her large desk — I have a bit of desk envy — and she hands me a piece of paper.

"My schedule for this week. I have one event on Friday evening that I will need an escort for. A ball organised by the Jewellers' Guild. Some of their members have donated to causes close to my heart, so I need to make an appearance. I have made you an appointment with my personal tailor for tomorrow afternoon. That way, your dress should be ready by Friday."

"Dress?" I gulp. "I suppose a suit or even jumpsuit is out of the question?"

"It is indeed. I'll make sure though that your dress will have pockets for weapons. Or maybe you prefer wearing sheaths underneath? You can discuss that with the tailor. I've given her some general instructions of what you need, but you'll be able to talk to her about the details."

Urgh. I hate dresses. When I need to shift while wearing one, it usually ends up too tight when I shift back. I did it once and it had changed shape so much that my boobs were on full display. No thanks.

I glance over her schedule. There are several other meetings this week, but they all take place here in the town hall. If we establish an efficient security, I might not need to be present for them.

"This one," Bethany says loudly and empties one of the bottles in one go.

I suppress any inkling of doubt that tries to creep up on me. She knows her stuff. No need to worry.

Lady Lara watches her curiously. She reminds me of a scientist studying one of her subjects. The thought makes a cold shiver run down my back. No, she's not one of them. Unless my instincts are completely wrong, she's one of the good guys. She may be very intense, but her heart's in the right place. That's my first impression, anyway. Time will tell if I was right. Everyone has some skeletons in their closet, but not all of them were murdered and put there by the owner of the closet.

When nothing happens to Bethany, Lady Lara smiles. "Well done. Can you name the poisons?"

"Yellownut, Pauper's Envy and this one was just water

with some elderflower syrup. Delicious, by the way. Do you have the recipe?"

The mayor laughs. "I like you. And yes, it's my grandmother's recipe. I shall write it down for you later. Now, it's time for you to meet the kitchen staff."

She walks around her desk and presses on one of several buttons lined up in a row.

"The cook will be with us shortly. She'll show you the kitchens and storerooms in the basement. Take a look around and make me a list of suggestions and improvements. Money isn't an issue."

Bethany smiles, her excitement evident. "My pleasure."

Lennox arrives at the same time as the cook. Like a gentleman, he opens the door for her.

She's a wisp of a woman; small, thin, frail looking. I wouldn't have imagined a cook to look like her, but her apron shows her profession. Maybe her cooking is so bad that she doesn't like to eat it herself?

"Bella, thanks for coming so quickly," Lady Lara greets her. "These are the people I told you about. Miss Bethany will accompany you to the kitchens to inspect if any improvements can be made. Please show her around. Take your time, I won't need lunch today. Miss Feln and I will be going out for lunch."

"We will?" I blurt.

Lara smiles at me. "We will indeed. I've not spent any time away from the town hall or my own house since the last assassination attempt. Now that I have you, it's time to show myself in public again. Besides, there's this lovely little restaurant by the river. You'll love it; their caviar is to die for."

CHAPTER NINE

I thought going for lunch would be boring, but Lady Lara is great company. She's interested in pretty much every topic we touch on, and she proves her intelligence and wit again and again. I have to admit to myself that I like being around her. Never thought I'd say that about someone as far removed from my life as her. Throughout our conversation, I try to drop hints about the supernatural, to coax her into admitting she knows about us. She's either too clever or she really doesn't know anything. Either is possible. One thing is for sure, I'll never underestimate her. From the stories she tells me, many have done that before, especially men. None of them has made it as far in their careers as she has.

If I were younger and in need of a role model, Lady Lara would be my woman of choice. I may have developed a slight crush on her. Not a romantic one. No, I don't think I swing that way. Although if she offered...no. Let's not go there. Three guys are completely enough to satisfy me. It's already hard to find time for them all. But maybe I should introduce Lily to Lady Lara. I can imagine they'd be perfect for each other. Yes, that will be my mission now. Save her from assassins and get her to fall in love with Lily.

I realise what I just thought. Am I going in heat again? Please, no. The last time was bad enough and I still don't know why it was so intense. If it happens again, I'll lock myself into a room until it's over. No lusting after my mates. No embarrassing myself.

"Are you enjoying the chocolate mousse?"

I startle and stare at my spoon that's been hovering above the dessert for the past minute while I was busy making plans for Lady Lara's love life. I quickly take a spoonful of the mousse and make a bit of a show of how much I enjoy it. Not that I have to act much. It truly is delicious. This entire meal has been amazing. If I were less stingy, I'd go here again, but alas, I don't like spending this much money on food. After all, all this food will mix in my stomach and then end up in the toilet just like the cheap meals I usually eat.

Lara leans back in her chair and smiles. "It feels good to get out and about again. I've been cooped up for too long. I know I shouldn't have let them frighten me, but it's hard to be confident in public when you know there are people out to kill you. It makes me lose my appetite."

"I'm not surprised. What I'm wondering though is why you didn't go on the offensive?"

"Because that wouldn't just go against my moral compass, but I also don't know who exactly has been sending the assassins. I have a whole list of people who're working against me, but most of them use political means to try and silence me. I'm not sure who of them would be ruthless enough to actually send someone to kill me."

I nod, even though I don't agree with her. If I was in her shoes, I'd have them all killed, or at least threatened enough to make them reconsider their position. I guess that's why she's a politician and I'm an assassin. I'd suck at being this restrained.

A couple enters the restaurant and all eyes turn to them. The man wears a black silk suit, while the woman's dress sparkles with sequins. The light from the three chandeliers reflects on her dress, making her seem radiant, as if she's just stepped out of a fairytale. Her long blonde hair reaches to her waist. No idea how often she has to brush it each day to keep it untangled. Definitely not a hairstyle for an assassin. Or anyone with a job that requires moving around.

The man looks around the room until he spots us. He lifts a hand in greeting.

Lady Lara sighs. "We should have left earlier. Now we're stuck with him."

"Who is he?" I whisper.

"The police chief. And yes, I know he doesn't look like it." She chuckles darkly. "I doubt he's ever set foot in a police station in all his life. He more or less inherited the title. Money, you see? Luckily, most of his officers are good enough to keep this town's police force running without his guidance. I've been trying to get rid of him but he's powerful."

She stops whispering when the couple come closer. The woman stares at me, her nose wrinkled as if she expects me to smell. Arrogant bitch. I may not be wearing a sequin dress but at least I'm not clutching a man's arm like he's the centre of my world. I'm my own woman.

"Lawrence, Lydia, such a pleasure to see you," Lady Lara says with a fake smile. "We were just about to leave, but do come and join us."

"If it's no trouble," the man says with an equally plastered smile. "And who's your charming companion?"

"Miss Feln is new to the city, so I decided to show her

my favourite restaurant," the mayor responds.

Lawrence frowns slightly, clearly disappointed with her vague reply.

"Welcome to Attenburgh," Lydia says loudly. Her fake smile is the worst of all of them. "Where are you from? A small village, I presume? Somewhere without access to proper tailors?"

"Lydia," her husband admonishes, but the way he looks at me shows he agrees with her. Stuck-up arses.

"I've lived in many places," I hedge. "But I really like Attenburgh so far. The people are so friendly, so welcoming."

Lady Lara snorts. I stare at her. I didn't expect her to react to my statement in that way. It makes me like her even more.

"Oh yes, we're known for being a very welcoming city," Lydia says cheerily, completely unaware of the sarcasm.

Lawrence looks pained as she starts talking about how nice people in Attenburgh are. I want to roll my eyes. This woman is completely out of touch with reality.

"Darling, why don't you choose something nice from the menu?" he interrupts her after a while.

I want to kick that patronising bastard in the balls.

He turns to Lady Lara. "I've been wanting to talk to you. I think we should have a chat about the police force's budget. Things are moving in the right direction since I took over, but with the current means, not all the changes I want to do are possible."

"And what changes are those?"

"A new police academy to make sure only the best are selected to serve our town. Better pensions for the officers who retire early. An extension of the current jail since they're running out of space in there."

"Yes, that was something *I* wanted to discuss with *you*,"

the mayor says pointedly. "You've imprisoned twice as many citizens as the previous police chief. Has crime suddenly doubled in Attenburgh or am I missing something?"

"No, but not all the crimes were pursued properly in the past. Criminals were let off too easily. I know my predecessor had some grand ideas about rehabilitation and community outreach, but the only message these people understand is being put under lock and key. You're very welcome to visit the jail and have a look around. After, I'm sure you'll agree that we need more funding."

"I might do that, actually," Lady Lara responds.

Lawrence's face remains stoic, but his heartbeat increases. He's not a happy bunny. I bet he imagined this conversation to go differently, ending with him having more money in his pockets. I hate people like him. I bet the increased pensions he wants would go to his friends and supporters rather than to ordinary police officers. I'd bet my last crumb of catnip that this man is corrupt. Maybe he's the one who's tried to kill the mayor? He'd certainly have the necessary connections.

"Darling, which wine would you like?" Lydia asks, seemingly unaware of the conversation going on around her.

"You choose," he mutters distractedly. "As long as it goes well with the lobster."

She smiles sweetly and continues to immerse herself in the menu. Pathetic. All wines taste the same. Grapes. Fermented grapes. Whoever had the idea to just let grapes rot for a while and then sell them for a lot of money? It doesn't make sense. It must have been someone rich with a lot of influence who managed to convince his posh friends that wine is a luxury drink. Silly people. I'll stick to proper drinks. Like tea.

Lady Lara gets up in one fluid, elegant movement. "We shall leave you to your lobster. I'm needed at the town hall."

Lawrence - I still don't know his last name - is clearly not pleased with us leaving, but there's nothing he can do about it. His wife ignores us, completely focused on the wine list. Mouse brain.

As soon as we're out of the restaurant, Lara takes a deep breath.

"Finally. I thought I'd have to make up an emergency, but he did let us go without the need for that. It's a first. He's like an octopus that doesn't want to let his prey go. Even if the prey is about to devour him."

I grin at her. "Making plans for his disposal?"

"You bet. But not the way you think. Shall we make a bet? I wager that I can get him out of his office within a month. Without bloodshed."

"What happens if you're wrong?"

Her smile turns predatory. "Then I'll leave him to you. No questions asked should something befall him. An accident. A mysterious illness. You get my gist."

"Oh, I definitely get it. A month, you say? How about we make it a little harder? Two weeks?"

"If I didn't know any better I'd say that you want to kill someone."

I shrug. "Luckily, you know better."

She raises her eyebrows, a silent message that she knows more about my past life than she lets on. Or maybe I'm not very good at passing as a normal person. I've been an assassin all my life and while I'm good at hiding in the shadows, I've rarely had to hide my personality. I suck at being a good, nice human. Cats aren't nice. That's an insult for any feline.

Lara sighs. "I guess it's time to go back to the office. Let's see if your friends have made any progress."

"Employees," I correct automatically. I may have finally reached the stage where I can admit to myself that they're my friends, but I don't want the outside world to know that. I have a reputation. True, not here, where nobody knows me, but I don't intend to ruin it with useless sentimentality before it's even been established. Assassins don't have friends. Business owners don't befriend their employees.

She grins at me. "Whatever you say. What shall I call you? An employee? A contractor?"

"Adviser. Head Adviser, with the others being the junior advisers. Something like that."

"Then I shall put that on your name badges. Although I think Bethany quite liked being called the Mistress of Poisons."

"Yes, I believe she did. She's a little vain sometimes, but she's the best at her job. She's saved my life more than once with her antidotes. And her poisons are to die for."

"I bet they are. I shall let you know if I'm ever in need of one. But you know already, I prefer to deal with problems my way. With diplomacy, wit and a bit of gentle blackmail."

"Blackmail, huh? Tell me more."

Lady Lara chuckles. "You'd like that, wouldn't you. Maybe another time. I don't want to share all my secrets at once. If this continues as well as it's going, then we'll have lots of time to exchange stories."

That means she likes having me around, right? I don't quite know what to do with that. People usually tell me to fuck off, or they never get the chance because I've already killed them.

This is new. Let's hope I don't mess it up.

Both Lennox and Bethany are waiting for us at the town hall's reception area. They look bored and hungry. Oops. Maybe I should have brought them some food. But then, they're both adults who should be able to look after themselves.

All three of us accompany Lara up to the fourth floor and into her office. She takes a seat behind her gorgeous desk while Bethany and Lennox take two of the more basic chairs. I stay standing, leaning against one of the panelled walls.

"I've sat for long enough today," I explain when Lady Lara raises an eyebrow at me.

She shrugs and leans forward, her elbows on the table, as she studies my employees.

"Lennox, let's begin with you. What's the security situation of my town hall?"

He clears his throat. "If you don't mind me being frank, it's not good. You don't have enough guards and the ones you have aren't trained well. I was able to sneak into the building and up to this floor a solid six times without being detected. And I intentionally made a lot of noise the final time. Nobody spotted me. The receptionist is the only person who seems interested in who enters and leaves the town hall. To be honest, I'd replace all the current guards with new ones. Training the old ones will probably take longer, since many of them will be stuck in their ways. I bet several of them are in the pockets of other people, too, judging from their attire. One of them wears a watch that must cost a lot more than he earns as a simple guard. If you want, I can look into all their backgrounds and situations, but it would be easier to just let them all go."

Lady Lara purses her lips. "I see what you mean, but I wouldn't want to leave them without a job, especially if they've worked for the town for a long time. I shall make a few calls to see if any other public buildings need new guards. That would shake up the status quo without the town hall employees losing their jobs. Or maybe they could transfer to the police force. Lawrence wants more resources, so I shall give them to him."

Again, I'm impressed. She's in charge of the entire city, yet she takes the time to make plans for the lives of lowly guards. How on Earth did she get this far in politics when most of her peers will be the complete opposite? Her compassion should be a weakness, yet for her, it's turned into a strength.

"Is something wrong with my face?" she suddenly asks.

"Uhm, no, why?"

"Because you're staring at me weirdly."

"Oh. Sorry. No weird staring intended."

She laughs. "Don't worry, I'm used to it. You don't become a woman in my position if you can't deal with some strange looks. Even my cat sometimes stares at me as if I'm a stranger. Or a weirdo."

My heart beats faster. She's even more amazing than I thought.

"You've got a cat?"

"Yes, Minka. She's an old lady, lazing around on the sofa all day. She's got arthritis, is blind in one eye, but she still struts around like she owns the world. She no longer goes outside, but she rules my house with an iron paw. If ever a mouse dared to enter my home…it wouldn't be alive for long."

I exchange a look with Lennox. We've got ourselves a cat lover. How perfect. I'll make sure to send one of Ryker's cats to make contact with Minka. Or maybe I'll do it myself. I haven't shifted in too long. Even if Minka doesn't leave Lady Lara's home, it's still good to have her on our side. If ever something happens to Lara, Minka could alert other cats in the area who could in turn notify me.

And the best thing about this is that Lara will never know. She won't feel watched in her own house. She's already used to her cat giving her strange looks – same as all cat owners.

Not owners, I correct myself. I'm using human language. Cats can't be owned. They're goddesses with human servants. They own their humans, but they're too clever to let them know that. Manipulation is a skill every kitten is born with.

Lara sighs. "Let's get back to business. Lennox, please go through our current guard roster and see if any of them can be kept on. Then make a list of what you're looking for in new guards so we can publish some job adverts. After recruitment, you can come up with a training programme for them. Until all that is sorted, I'd quite like you to stay around, Kat."

I nod, the sound of clinking coins ringing in my ears.

"Of course. I'll be at your disposal as much as I can. My other employee, Gryphon, can take my place in emergencies too."

Bethany snickers when I call my lover my employee. I bet she'll tell him as soon as we get home. As long as he takes his revenge in bed and not by other means...fine by me.

Lady Lara turns the Mistress of Potions. "Bethany, did you find anything that can be improved in the kitchens?"

"Yes, a lot." She pulls a crumpled piece of paper from her pocket. "I've made a list. The ones with the stars are the most essential improvements. But to be honest, the whole situation is one big poisoning waiting to happen. Most folks in the kitchens know where their supplies come from. Food is stored in rooms that aren't locked. Anyone could go in there and poison it."

Lara sighs. "As I feared. I'll pass the list on to my assistants and I'll ask you to come back once the changes have been implemented." Her smile turns evil. "Maybe do a little demonstration to see if everyone is sticking to the rules. Not a lethal poison, of course, but something that will leave a memory."

I swoon mentally. She wants to poison her staff. Now that's amazing. Maybe I should do that, too, as a test run. Or maybe not. Bethany is better at poisons than me and her revenge would be painful.

After some more discussions on what to change, Lady Lara lets us go. I'm strangely exhausted. Too much socialising. I need a run, on my own.

"You two go home, I'll get some exercise."

Lennox looks at me knowingly. "I'd join you, but I shouldn't shift so soon after the full moon."

"I get it. Don't worry. I need some alone time anyway."

Bethany grins. "Too many people. I agree. Those

bitches in the kitchens were so unfriendly that I may have exchanged the sugar with the salt. They should be glad I didn't poison them. Believe me, I was tempted."

I chuckle. Bethany is proving a lot of restraint. Fascinating. Maybe that's what she's needed; a job for people other than me. I don't have enough authority when it comes to her. She does what she wants and only follows my orders when there's enough of an incentive. This will be good for her.

I nod to myself. It will be good for all of us.

As soon as I'm out of the city, I shift. I groan in pleasure as my limbs lengthen and fur erupts on my skin. My mind turns lighter, simpler somehow, while my senses increase and I become one with my surroundings.

A purr breaks from my chest. The evening sun warms my black fur and I'm tempted to just lie down and take a nap. I shouldn't be out yet, not in daylight, but I couldn't hold back any longer. I've repressed my cat for too long and it's time to let it run free.

My paws are almost soundless on the soft grass. I extend and retract my claws while I walk, stretching those muscles. I don't have them as a human and I never remember how good it feels to exercise them until I'm shifted. Of course, it would be even more satisfying to rake my claws over my prey's body, but you can't have it all.

I start running, faster and faster, flying across the landscape like a black lightning bolt. The wind ruffles my fur, bits of earth hit my face, the smell of life fills me. This is heaven.

I don't pay much attention to where I'm going. Away from the city, across endless fields, over meadows and marshy grasslands. Every time my paws leave the ground, I'm flying, weightlessly, free. I never feel as free as when I'm shifted. Maybe I'm truly a cat and my human form is just a disguise. A by-product of the experiments they did on me.

By the time I reach the edge of the woods, the sun has disappeared behind the horizon. The air is turning cooler, but my fur keeps out the cold. In fact, I'm a little too hot from all the running. I slow down to a trot and walk into the forest.

Hundreds of birds warn each other when I cross the treeline. It's an old forest, full of moss and thick roots. I doubt many humans come here. With the way the trees have grown, twisting around each other, in all directions, it must not be worth it for logging.

I stop and breathe in the air, thick with smells. Bird droppings, animal piss, rotting leaves. And above that, flowers, the refreshing smell of a nearby stream, blood.

Blood. I sniff again. Deer, if I'm not mistaken.

I stalk in the direction of the scent, all my senses on high alert. The birds have stopped singing, as if they're watching me, waiting to see what's going to happen next.

When I get closer, sounds begin to filer through the undergrowth. A pitiful whine, the equivalent of a human sob. Definitely a deer. And then, the harsh laughter of a human male. I freeze. I shouldn't let any human see me. A panther in the forest would raise eyebrows. Panthers live in faraway countries, not here. As a child, I was able to pass as a large cat, but those times are long over. There's no mistaking me for what I am.

The deer whimpers again. It's in pain, but the human seems in no hurry to stop it. A hunter, I assume. What is he waiting for? Just kill it and go home.

I grit my teeth and continue to prowl towards the

sound. The deer's pain tears at my heartstrings. The poor thing is suffering.

The smell of blood is making my body tense up. I'm going into hunter mode, but when I see what's happening, the little fawn isn't my prey. No, it's the human who's toying with the injured animal. He's got a knife in his hands and is carving a pattern into the deer's flank, causing blood to paint its spotted fur red. He's not doing this to provide his family with food. He's torturing the fawn.

Now, I love torture as much as the next assassin, but this is wrong. This is not a hardened criminal who needs to be taught a lesson, or an informant unwilling to part with crucial information. This is an innocent animal that's done nothing wrong.

I growl and launch myself at the human. I'm too fast for him to react. His knife falls to the ground as I topple him over. My fangs press against his throat for just long enough to see the fear in his eyes, then I bite down hard. I rip out his throat, enjoying the squelching sound as blood pours from his open neck. I lick my maw. Human blood. I forgot how good it made me felt. One of the reasons why I've not shifted, why I've not killed. It scares me how good it tastes. I rub my face against the wound. The man is still alive; his blood is still pumping. His heartbeat is almost inaudible though. He won't last much longer, and fresh blood is so much better...

The fawn whimpers again, pulling me from my blood-induced haze. I force myself to step away from the dying human and face the little deer. It's bleeding, but it doesn't seem to be in mortal danger.

If I was a proper cat, I'd kill it. Not just because that would stop its pain, but also because that's what predators do. Instead, I lick its wounds, knowing that my saliva will increase the speed of healing. The fawn stops whimpering and stares at me in surprise. Its eyes are massive, black orbs filled with cuteness. Oh my. I've fallen for yet another baby animal. My housemates are going to kill me.

I sigh and gently lift the deer by the scruff of its neck. Looks like I got myself another pet.

CHAPTER ELEVEN

By the time I get back to the house, night has fallen, concealing me from curious eyes. Even so, as soon as I entered the town, three cats greeted me. They've been following me ever since, throwing me disdainful looks. They know it's bad to fall for your food. But whenever the fawn whimpers or makes another pitiful sound, my heart aches and I just can't help it. I want to make sure it's safe.

Ryker greets me on the doorstep.

"I wasn't quite sure what to make of the news the cats were giving me," he chuckles. "I thought they were having a laugh, but no, you're actually carrying a deer in your mouth like a cat would her kittens. What happened?"

I can't talk with the fawn held in my jaws, so I strut past him, swinging my hips seductively. Well, kind of. Not sure I can do seductive hip-swinging while shifted.

I walk straight to the kitchen and gently lower the fawn onto the tiled floor. Lily would kill me if I got bloodstains on the living room carpet. She almost stabbed Bethany for dripping tomato sauce on it. Blood would likely face even harsher punishment.

I shift, regretting the decision as soon as I'm human again. I wasn't shifted for nearly long enough.

Ryker has followed me, his amusement obvious.

"A human hurt it," I explain indignantly. "I couldn't just leave it there."

"You could have stopped it from suffering," he retorts. "What are we supposed to do with a deer?"

Benjamin storms into the kitchen.

"What's-" He sees the deer, and his eyes and mouth widen almost comically. "Is that a-"

"Yes," I sigh. "It's a fawn. And no, it isn't going to be dinner. And yes, if you want, you can take care of it along with your kittens."

He gapes at me. "I can do that? Really?"

"It's not like I have the time to look after a baby animal. I've got a mayor to babysit, that's a lot harder. How did you even know what was happening?"

He grins and points at the white fluff ball rubbing against his legs.

"Nyx told me that something was up. I just didn't know what, but it seemed important." Benjamin shrugs. "I assumed it would be you hurt, or one of the others. I certainly didn't expect this."

I sigh again. "Neither did I. All I wanted was a nice, relaxing run through the woods. Instead, I ended up with this. Any idea what fawns eat? Meat? Catnip? Milk?"

Benjamin rolls his eyes. "I'm glad you've left it in my care. Is it a male or a female?"

"Female," Ryker replies in my stead. "Definitely. I can smell it."

Okay then. Why not, I guess. He's probably used to my female smell.

"Can you talk to her?" Benjamin asks. "Or does your animal whispering skills only work for cats?"

"Felines only. I'm sure the fawn has understood by now that we mean her no harm, but I doubt she can understand our words. They're not as clever as cats."

He sighs. "I guess that would have been too easy. I'll just have to manage without translations. Do you have a name for her yet?"

"A name?"

He does his all-familiar eye roll. "I guess not. You really aren't good with pets. I shall call her Willow."

I shrug. "She's yours now, call her whatever you want. And make sure the cats don't play too rough with it. It'll take a while for those wounds to heal."

Benjamin nods. "I'll keep her in my room for now. Maybe Bethany has some herbs that might help with the healing. Otherwise you can lick her."

"I'm not Ivy."

"No, but it's still more effective than human spit."

Ryker chuckles. "I love it when you two bicker. It's adorable."

I glare at him. "I don't bicker."

"Yes, you do. Can we take this conversation somewhere else? The bedroom, for example? Gryphon and Lennox are already up there. I doubt they're sleeping."

My ovaries clench. I doubt that too. All three of us are home at the same time. That happens rarely. I should take advantage of it, but I'm also tired from all the running.

Benjamin gently picks up the fawn and leaves the room without another word. I think he doesn't like it when the guys and I get too personal. Fine by me. I like my privacy.

"Let's go upstairs," I say with a sigh. "But no promises. I need a break."

Ryker grins at me. "A massage, maybe? That might revitalise you."

Oh. Now that's an offer. His massages are legendary. If

I could, I'd spend all day in bed with his hands kneading my muscles. No idea how he knows how to do that, having spent all his life as a cat, but he's amazing at it.

He takes my hand and pulls me out of the kitchen. We leave a small puddle of deer blood on the floor; a gift to whoever will come into the room next. Nice of us, right? The people in this house love surprises, whether it's a bodiless head in the fridge or a stack of new poisons.

"By the way, Caitlin has been hard at work figuring out the puzzle," he says while we climb the stairs. "She's close. Well, I think she's already solved it, but she wants to impress you, so she wants to be really sure."

That's adorable. My little sister wants to impress me. To be honest, she impresses me every single day with how she adapts to normal life without a single word of complaint. She dutifully takes her daily potion that keeps her sane and away from the influence of the Pack. In a city full of sirens, her mental vulnerability could become a threat, so I'm glad she doesn't need any babysitting in this matter.

"I'll talk to her tomorrow. The mayor won't need me until the afternoon, so I'll have the morning to deal with our treasure hunt."

He laughs. "Lennox seems to have been very impressed by Lady Lara. If I didn't know that you're the only female in his life, I'd think he's got a crush on her."

I growl. "No way."

"Don't worry, I think it's just professional admiration. She sounds like a formidable woman."

"That she is. I have no idea how she managed to rise so high without losing her humanity and compassion. She's not a normal politician at all. She actually cares for the people of this town and it's clear that she wants to make everyone's life better, not just that of the rich and powerful."

"That sounds like a rare politician indeed. I can't wait to meet her."

"If you want, you can come along tomorrow. I've told her that I'll introduce her to all the members of my team, so that's a good a day as any. She already knows Lennox and Bethany, although I'm not sure she'll need to meet Lily. Her skills aren't as easy to apply to the mayor's work."

Ryker snorts. "Unless she needs lessons in seducing her fellow politicians."

"I don't think she needs lessons in that. She's gorgeous, intelligent, witty, funny,..."

I let my voice trail off when I realise how infatuated I sound. Like a teenager experiencing her first crush. No, I don't feel about her that way. No. Definitely not.

He looks at me curiously. "Now I really can't wait to see her in person. It takes a lot to impress you."

I realise we've stopped in front of my bedroom door. I sniff the air. Neither of the other guys are in there; they've both retreated to their own rooms. Now I need to decide whether to invite them to mine or turn this into a quiet, relaxed, solitary night.

I roll my shoulders and realise how tense I still am. The running made it better, but I didn't get enough exercise. I need to relax, and the man next to me is the perfect way to do so.

"Did you mention a massage?" I mutter and open my bedroom door, pulling him inside with me.

"I did indeed. Where would you like it?"

I frown. "On the bed, obviously. I'm not lying on the floor."

"I wasn't talking about where in this room."

He puts his hands on my hips and pulls me close. "I

could massage you here..." His hands wander down until they cup my arse. "Or here." He squeezes and I jump a little. Ryker laughs and moves his hands up again, running them up my spine. "Or just your back?" He leaves one of his hands between my shoulder blades, but puts his other on one breast. "Or here..."

I moan softly as he starts massaging my boob. My nipples grow hard. I hate myself for reacting to him like that. So needy. Like I need him to feel good. Which isn't true. I can be happy without him. But now that he's here, his hands all over my body...

I stop thinking and focus on the sensations of his touch. When it's not quite enough, I pull off my shirt and bra, presenting him my naked body as his instrument.

He picks me up and gently lays me on the bed. He somehow manages to pull my trousers down, with a bit of wiggling on my part. Now I'm naked, bare before him, vulnerable. I trust him, though. He's one of three people who I'd let them put me in such a position. No weapons. No poisons. Not even a lethal hairpin. Just me, without anything to hide behind.

A shiver runs down my back. This is so unlike the old Kat. Whenever I spent a night with a man, I'd not take off all my clothes. I always had a knife in reaching distance. With Ryker though, I don't care about my daggers. All I care about is his touch.

He kneels next to me on the bed and starts massaging my shoulders, finding all the little knots and tense spots that have built up over the past week. He's not exactly gentle, but that's how I like it. I couldn't bear it if he just sat there and stroked my skin like an idiot.

When he moves down my body, my nipples harden again. My shoulders are a non-sexual place, but now that he's nearing my bum, I remember that he's my mate, that

I'm naked and that he wants me. And I want him. Patience, kitty. Let him do his job first. This is foreplay, in a way.

He gently pushes a finger between my arse cheeks. I stop breathing.

"How about here?"

When I don't react, he proceeds further until he reaches my wet core. This time, I moan.

"I knew you'd like a massage there," he chuckles and pushes a finger into me.

I relax. Yes, this is just what I needed.

CHAPTER TWELVE

I wake up next to a big fluffy cat. Ryker must have shifted at some point during the night. What the heck? He's not done that before.

I nudge him until he blinks open his yellow eyes.

"Why did you shift?"

In response, he purrs and closes his eyes again. How frustratingly cute. Although it's a bit weird lying naked next to an overgrown cat. Ryker, the man, the male who pleasured me for hours last night, is somewhere in there, covered in far too much fur. As a panther, my fur is nowhere near as fluffy as his. I prefer it that way. Less hair to leave as evidence at crime scenes.

I check my watch. I've still got a couple of hours until I need to head for the town hall. Ryker will definitely have to shift for that, but for now, I let him be. If I hadn't spent several hours as a cat yesterday, I'd join him. But no, I need to preserve my energy for emergencies. Shifting too often is exhausting and makes it more and more painful with every shift.

I roll onto my side and run a hand through his bushy

fur. He purrs again, a rumble that makes the entire mattress tremble. I smile and scratch him between the ears, just the way he likes it. He gave me the best massage of my life last night, so now I'm repaying the favour. Just in a more innocent way.

"Kat, are you up?" Caitlin shouts from below. Urgh, I hate my sensitive hearing sometimes.

Ryker pushes his head against my hand, nudging me to get up.

"Easy for you to say," I grumble. "You can stay here and sleep."

He grins at me, showing me his sharp fangs.

"Bastard."

I get dressed in a flash and leave Ryker to his morning nap. Caitlin and Lily are in the kitchen, eating something that looks like porridge but smells like something I don't want to get anywhere near my mouth. We really need a cook.

"Morning," Lily says cheerily. "Did we wake you?"

"No, a purring cat did."

I sit down on one of the bar stools that Bethany got at a flea market just after we moved here.

"Did one of them get into your room?" Caitlin asks. "Did you forget to close the door?"

I grimace. "No, I let him in last night. He just wasn't a cat when I fell asleep."

Realisation flashes across her face. As always, I'm startled by how much she looks like me, except that I'd never have such an easily readable expression.

Lily puts a mug of tea in front of me. "You'll need this."

I frown at her. "Why?"

"Because of what Caitlin has discovered. Do you want some food too?"

I wrinkle my nose. "Not if the food is whatever you're having."

Lily sighs. "It's not all that bad. I remembered to take it off the hob on time today. It's barely burned."

"I'll make myself something later," I say, fully intending to draw on my secret catnip supply as soon as Lily isn't looking. "Caitlin, you solved the puzzle?"

She nods proudly. "I did. It wasn't all that hard once I figured out the pattern. The language in the book wasn't actually a different language, just syllables replaced with others. Like a secret code where you replace one letter with another, except that they used entire letter combinations to make it look more like an actual language. Pretty clever, but I solved it. Once I could read the message in the book, the rest was pretty easy to figure out."

I take a sip of tea, glad that's one thing Lily can make. I would have added more milk, but I hold my tongue and let Caitlin continue.

"It's a heist," she blurts. "A real diamond heist. There's going to be a big Jewellers' Guild event soon where they're going to have a big, expensive diamond on show. Priceless. Unbelievably expensive. We'd be rich for the rest of our lives."

I swallow hard. Lady Lara mentioned that ball. I'm supposed to accompany her there. I think I can see a conflict of interest coming up.

"So the whole mysterious challenge is stealing the diamond?" I ask Caitlin.

She nods enthusiastically. "Yes. They even give us helpful pointers on where the diamond will be kept and predictions of how strong the security will be. They'll also take the diamond and pay us for it once we retrieve it. I guess that's good; it must be hard to sell a massive diamond without arousing suspicion."

"That all sounds good, but why aren't they stealing it themselves? Do you have any idea who's behind all this?"

"No idea. Attenburgh's shady underworld? Although it feels to me like this is less about the money and more of a game. Maybe someone in the upper class got bored and decided to have some fun, while also taking revenge on some poor jeweller. But as I said, I don't really know. None of the items we found show an indication of who put them there."

Mmhm. Interesting. I don't usually take jobs by anonymous contacts. It can be too easy for someone to just decide to have someone killed when they don't have to face the assassin themselves. It's why I'm the best. I don't kill just anyone. Only the people who deserve it.

"Do you think we should do it?" Caitlin asks. Her eyes are almost glowing with excitement. It's clear that she wants to continue with this wild jewel chase.

"I'm not going to be able to get involved," I say hesitantly. "I'll be at that event, but I'll be guarding Lady Lara. While wearing a dress. I doubt I'll have much opportunity to go and steal diamonds. However, I could probably get you in, either as my assistant or open a door somewhere."

Caitlin rolls her eyes. "I don't need you to open a door. I can do that myself."

She's right. Sometimes, I like to forget that she grew up in a similar way to me. We were both trained as weapons. Locked doors are no challenge to either of us.

"I want to play too," Lily interrupts. "I've never done a heist before."

"Did I hear heist?" Benjamin asks, entering the kitchen. He's accompanied by three cats, one of them Nyx. She follows him wherever he goes. I think she's secretly in love with him.

"Yes, you did." Caitlin quickly explains her findings.

The more he hears, the happier Benjamin looks. "I'm in. You need a thief if you want it to succeed."

"I can steal a diamond by myself," Caitlin protests, but I shut her up with a flick of my hand.

"If you want to do it, you'll take Benjamin along with you. He's the best thief I've ever met and you might be able to learn something from him."

Caitlin gives me a grumpy look, but stays quiet. Wise girl. She should be happy that I'm letting her have all the fun. I really want to do it myself. A diamond heist...I love diamonds, especially stealing them. It's no surprise that we've come across this challenge in Attenburgh. This town is full of rich people who can afford to have jewels lying around.

Benjamin smiles at me. "What are we doing with it afterwards? Are you really going to sell it to whoever created the treasure hunt?"

I shrug. "I haven't decided yet. It's a bit boring to just hand over the diamond to them. Maybe we'll keep it for a while until everyone forgets about the theft, before selling it ourselves. We might make more that way."

Benjamin's grin turns even wider. "I like that. I've already made some contacts here that could be useful. Or even better, we could sell it back home. Nobody would make the connection there. And it would give us an excuse to visit the cats there."

"The cats?" I laugh. "I'd be more interested in visiting my sisters."

"Yeah, those too. I guess they count as cats."

That boy is weird. He's human, but I bet he would give anything to be a shifter. The way he acts around the cats who've adopted him...it's a match made in heaven.

"How's the fawn?" I ask while he makes himself some coffee.

"The wounds have started to heal. She's been on my bed all night, moving as little as possible. I think she's still in quite a lot of pain. I'll go and get some food for Willow now. Need anything from the market?"

"Catnip?"

Lily elbows me in the side. "No drugs for you."

I groan. "Ouch. If there's no catnip, then at least bring some boring food. The fridge is looking pretty empty."

"Because you all eat too much," Lily complains. "Whenever I buy something, it's gone the next day."

"We're a lot of people," I say with a shrug. "And cats."

"We should get a garden and grow our own food," Caitlin says enthusiastically.

The rest of us stare at her. A garden? Who on Earth would think that of us make good gardeners? She's deluded. Probably trying to be more normal than she'll ever be. Bah. Ordinary people suck. Just like gardening. Mowing the grass, now that's a different matter. Killing grass at record speed...maybe I should invent some kind of mower for humans. Or not. That would take out all the fun out of a well-executed assassination.

I check my watch. Almost time to go. I better wake Ryker if he wants to come along.

I finish my tea and throw a longing look at the cupboard where I've got my catnip stashed.

Lily chuckled. "It's no longer there."

"What?!"

"I've put it into a safe place where neither you nor the kittens will be tempted."

I gape at her. "You touched my catnip?"

"Yes. And you should be glad that I did. I don't want you to go all crazy again."

"I didn't go crazy," I mutter, still angry at her. "That was just me giving in to my instincts."

"As I said. Crazy. I'll keep it hidden for emergencies. If one of us dies, you may have some to cheer you up."

Benjamin clears his throat. "Are you expecting any deaths in the near future?"

Lily shrugs. "It's always good to plan ahead."

I hate her so much.

Lady Lara ambushes me with the tailor. I'd hoped I'd get some reprieve before I'm turned into a needle cushion, but no such luck. I wish Ryker were here to give me mental support, but he won't get here until later. He needed to sort out a few cat things first.

The tailor is a tall, elegant woman wrapped in a cerulean silk costume that shows a lot of skin while also hiding all the important bits. Her black hair is styled into something that reminds me of a unicorn horn. So impractical.

Lady Lara smiles wickedly. "I've pulled your appointment forward a little since I have some last-minute work to do. Miss Quim will look after you. We've already discussed what you need, so you'll just need to stand there and look pretty."

I shoot her a glare. She knows exactly that I don't want to do this. Other people might be happy to get free tailored dresses as part of their job, but not me. Now, if they were to give me a new leather jumpsuit, I'd be far more inclined to purr with joy. Mine is getting old, but leather is expensive and it's hard to find someone to make me a new one without asking any silly questions. It's nobody's business why I need holes in my collar for poison darts and inbuilt sheaths for at least four daggers.

"Lovely to meet you," Miss Quim chirps. "Let's go to my studio and I'll have you measured up in no time."

I give Lady Lara one more glare, which she returns with an innocent smile. That woman is evil. In a good way.

The 'studio' turns out to be an empty office on the third floor that the tailor has transformed into a makeshift fitting room. Bundles of fabric are lined up on desks. Most of them are dark colours; at least I won't be forced to wear pink or white.

A small, bald man is waiting for us. He's wearing a bright green suit and a yellow scarf, but he doesn't look quite comfortable in his own skin. As if he's trying to portray something he's not.

"Meet Stephen, my assistant," Miss Quim introduces him. "He's new, but don't worry, he's come highly recommended. Rest assured that you won't be pricked by a single needle."

"That's reassuring," I reply dryly. "I prefer to do the pricking myself."

She gives me a confused look, but then plasters a smile on her face and beckons me to stand on the low round platform in the centre of the room. Reluctantly, I follow her instructions.

"Spread your arms a little, my dear. I need to see your waist."

I sigh and do as she says. Both she and Stephen walk around me, inspecting me from all angles. I've never been this uncomfortable in all my life. Their eyes bore into me, taking in every single flaw. I feel like they can see my scars even through my clothes. Those scars tell stories of my upbringing; memories painted on my skin to last forever. A few of them speak of close encounters with death. There's one small scar on the back of my neck where a knife once pierced my skin, almost reaching my spine.

"You're lovely," Miss Quim says in her chirpy, cheerful voice. "Easy to work with. When Lady Lara said she needed an outfit for her new female bodyguard, I expected someone burly, masculine, but you're perfect. I know exactly what dress I'll make for you."

I kind of wish I was how she imagined me. Maybe then she'd give me a shirt and trousers rather than a dress.

"Don't look so gloomy, it's going to be fun!"

I raise an eyebrow at her. Fun? I highly doubt it. Torture, more like. One of the first things I learned in my training is that mental torture is a lot more effective than physical. You can only cut off a limb once, but you can break their mind piece by piece, taking your time, playing with them. Now, I'm the victim who's being tortured with dresses.

"I'll need you to take off your clothes now," she continues. "I can't measure you properly like this. Stephen will leave the room for that, unless you want him to stay?"

Why on Earth would I want that?

I sigh. She takes that as a sign of approval and waves Stephen away. He hurries from the room without looking back. I wish I were in his position. I don't want to be here either.

Miss Quim looks at me expectantly. "Clothes off."

"Can't you-"

"No. I will get the measurements wrong otherwise and that would result in an ill-fitting dress. I've got a reputation and I won't risk it because you're shy."

"I'm not shy," I protest.

"Then why are you still dressed?"

A growl escapes me. Her eyes widen for a second, but she keeps her composure.

Looks like I don't have a choice. I pull my shirt over my head, take off my boots and wiggle out of my cargo trousers.

"You're pretty," she says while inspecting my body from all sides. "You should wear more flattering clothes."

"I prefer practical and durable," I retort. "Everything else tends to get in the way."

She shrugs as if that's a price worth paying for looking beautiful. I don't agree, but I better get this over with.

Miss Quim takes out a tape measure and starts assessing the length of my limbs. She doesn't make notes, so I assume she's got a good memory. Or this is just torture and she doesn't really need to do it.

"Relax," she says when she's done measuring my legs. "You're stiff as a corpse."

I'd love to turn you into a corpse, lady.

"I'll relax when we're done," I growl. "How much longer is this going to take?"

"As long as it has to. I'm going to make you the prettiest dress you've ever seen. While I'm measuring you, let's talk about your preferences."

"I have a say in this?"

"Of course. Lady Lara has given me quite detailed instructions, but there are still decisions to be made. What's your favourite colour?"

"Red, blood red. Or black."

"I'm afraid neither will work," Miss Quim says with a chuckle. "Black isn't worn unless you're at a funeral, and red would be too dramatic. You don't want to outshine some of the ladies of the high society. They might take it the wrong way. Since you're there as Lady Lara's bodyguard, you'll have to blend in while also reflecting her authority and high station. It's not an easy task but that's why she brought me in. I'm the best."

"You're not vain at all," I scoff.

"Just saying it as it is. Ask anyone in this town and they'll point you to me if they need an excellent tailor. How about green?"

I shrug. "Better than pink or yellow."

"I'm thinking a dark, emerald green, with panels of a lighter shade, maybe olive. Then a collar of dark seaweed green, decorated with small gemstones."

"Gemstones? Are you for real?"

She laughs. "They're well inside the budget Lady Lara gave me. Now, tell me, what are your requirements in terms of your job? I assume you'll be bringing weapons?"

I nod. "I'll need easy access to my knives. I've got sheaths that I can wear around my thighs and lower arms, but I'd need slits or something like that in the dress to reach them. I also like to have a couple of poison darts. They're easy to hide beneath a collar or inside a thick seam."

"That's no problem. Do you need pockets?"

"Pockets?" I cheer up immediately. "You can put pockets on a dress?"

Miss Quim laughs again. "Of course. This isn't the first time I've made a dress that's more than it seems at first glance. Recently, I've experimented with a new kind of fabric that is said to be stab-proof. I've used it for the bodice of the dress Lady Lara will be wearing on Friday. With a bit of lace as decoration it looks just like any other dress."

That's surprisingly clever. It's also good to know that Lady Lara will be protected by more than just myself. The dress won't save her if someone tries to poison her or cut her throat, but it's a start.

The tailor continues to prod and measure me, making me lift my arms into weird positions, all the while assessing every inch of me. I hate it. If Lady Lara didn't pay as much as she does, I'd run out of here, screaming. Or kill the tailor. Probably both.

When she's finally done, I breathe a dramatic sigh of relief. As soon as I've put on my clothes, Miss Quim calls for Stephen to return. He looks even more uncomfortable now than he did earlier. Something is strange about this man, but I can't quite put my finger on it. Maybe it's just me not being used to tailors and being measured like a sheep for slaughter, but I've learned to trust my instincts.

Miss Quim waves me over to the fabric-laden desks.

"Which one do you prefer? Not the colour, the fabric. They're all of the highest quality, obviously, but some people find this one here too sticky on their skin, for example."

I touch all the fabrics she points at, feeling a little silly. She puts so much effort into a single garment that will likely only be worn once or twice. Is that how people like her make a living? I'd die of boredom. I don't really care about the fabrics, so I put my hand on a random one that's closest to which I stand.

"This one."

She raises her perfectly manicured eyebrows. "Are you sure? This fabric is quite see-through, especially in bright lights."

"Ehm, I meant that one." I point at the dark red fabric next to it which looks more solid. Why can't this woman see that I couldn't care less? As long as she doesn't make me go to the event naked or in nothing but my underwear, I'll be fine. Yes, I'll grumble and complain, but in the end, it doesn't matter what I wear. It's all about Lady Lara's safety.

Miss Quim nods. "Then that's it. We'll accompany you back to Lady Lara and then I'll get started on making your dress."

Oh joy.

CHAPTER FOURTEEN

L ady Lara looks bored, but her expression brightens when we enter the room.

"All done?" she asks. I roll my eyes, but Miss Quim nods enthusiastically.

"I'll make her the best dress you've ever seen. Beautiful, practical, transforming."

"I don't need to be transformed," I mutter. "I like the way I am."

"Yes, yes," the tailor chatters dismissively. "Now if there's nothing else we can do for you, then I better get back to my studio so I can start creating the dress."

"Excuse me," Stephen suddenly says. "I think I made a mistake when measuring the mayor last week. May I quickly check the length of your arm, my lady?"

Lara frowns, but gives him a nod. "Go ahead, I was just about to finish anyway."

He inclines his head and steps forward, pulling some measuring tape from his pocket. Miss Quim looks confused. I tense up, my instinct screaming at me. Something bad is going on.

In a flash, I'm by Lady Lara's side, before Stephen can touch her.

"Step away from her," I growl.

"What's going-" Lara protests, but I cut her off. I snatch the tape from Stephen's hand, moving faster than a human should. I don't care; she's in danger. I can feel it all the way from my toes up into the tips of my hair.

Stephen freezes, his eyes wide. He seems unsure of what to do next. I take advantage of that and pull Lady Lara away from him. I push her behind me, out of harm's way, then inspect the measuring tape. It has a strange smell, even when inside its plastic casing.

I unravel it, careful not to touch the ends. Stephen isn't wearing any gloves, so it should be safe to pull it by its metal end. I give the tape a sniff. Fuck.

I let it fall to the ground and stalk towards Stephen, putting a hand around his throat.

"Why?" I hiss.

His eyes widen until they almost seem ready to jump from their sockets. He doesn't reply though. His lips are pressed together in a thin line, but his defiance seems weak. He's going to break under a bit of pressure.

"What's going on?" Lady Lara asks sharply.

"He tried to poison you," I growl, white patting Stephen down for weapons, just in case. "The measuring tape is laced with moonshade. One nick of your skin and you'd be at death's door ten hours later. And since it's hard to match the symptoms to this poison, nobody would have been the wiser."

I increase my hold on his throat. He gasps for air. I let him struggle. He may be about my height, but I'm a lot stronger than him. He should be grateful that I haven't let my claws out. I'd love to rake them across his skin, make him bleed, but we've got an audience who aren't aware of my true nature.

"Why?" I repeat. "You have exactly ten seconds to reply before I'll cut off your dick."

His lips quiver. Pathetic. If you want to kill someone, at least be brave enough to admit to it.

"Ten. Nine. Eight."

"Tell her now or I'll skewer you myself," the tailor shouts. "I have enough knitting needles with me to make it painful."

My opinion of her improves slightly. She seems genuinely angry and shocked at her assistant's betrayal. Of course, I'll have to investigate her background to see if she's in on it, if she has a reason to harm the mayor, but for now, I'll assume that Stephen is acting on his own.

"Seven. Six. Five. Four."

A tear runs down his face. I almost puke. He doesn't deserve to call himself an assassin. He's a weakling who played with poison and failed to achieve his target. Absolutely pathetic. He deserves to suffer for this, a lot.

"Three. Two."

I pull a knife from my belt and twirl it in my hand, making sure he sees exactly how sharp it is. A blunt knife would be more fun, but it doesn't work as well for threats.

"I..." he stammers, then decides differently and presses his lips together again. Idiot.

I run the blade across his cheek, leaving a red line. A single drop of blood falls onto his shirt, leaving a red stain on the pristine fabric.

"One."

His internal struggle is clear to see. Sweat beads on his forehead and his armpits have begun to stink. Just a tiny push and he'll break. Problem is, these weak-minded people can break in two ways. Either they submit to you and tell you everything they know, or they go crazy, break down and try to do something stupid. I've not quite decided which category Stephen falls into.

"That's it. You've had your chance. Ladies, would you mind relieving him of his trousers? I like to see where I cut. Less messy."

"Could you do this outside?" Lady Lara asks as if this is an everyday occurrence. "I only recently had this carpet cleaned."

"Is there a bathroom nearby?"

"Just around the corner. I'll make sure you stay undisturbed, even if there are screams."

I love how easily she plays along. Her voice is completely calm and collected. She's my perfect partner in crime. Pity she chose to become a politician on this side of the law.

"Stephen, tell her," Miss Quim pleads. "Don't make this worse than it already is."

She hasn't realised yet that her assistant won't make it out of here alive. Even if Lady Lara insists on giving him a fair trial, I won't let that happen. Accidents happen on the way to the police station. Or prisoners kill themselves in their cell. It wouldn't be the first time that I've made sure that justice is done. This man is a danger to others and with his incompetence, he might actually succeed in harming Lady Lara in future. He's so bad an assassin that he's almost good. His stupidity makes him harder to predict.

"I..."

I sigh. "Cat got your tongue?"

"I was paid," he whispers. His sweat has started to run down his face, leaving wet marks along his cheeks. Yuck. "They paid me to do it."

"Who?" I snap.

"None of your business."

I flick my knife and cut across his other cheek. He winces, but to my surprise he doesn't cry out. He's stopped struggling, his body strangely still. After all the quivering from earlier, this is a weird turn.

"What's going on?" I snarl. "Tell me now or lose your dick."

"It's tiny anyway, not much to lose," Miss Quim scoffs from behind me. Sounds like she has first-hand experience.

Stephen's lips curl into a smile. His eyes are no longer wide, but his pupils have increased in size as if he's on drugs. Something strange is going on and have no idea what. It makes me frustrated, which in turn means I get careless. That's never a good thing. I need to focus and stay alert. He didn't have any obvious weapons on him, but maybe I should have him strip just to be sure.

"Let's take you to the bathroom," I announce. "I want to see how tiny your dick really is."

"Brave words," he chuckles. I stare at him. His expression changes completely in a fraction of a second. Like someone else is taking over. His eyes are more intense, staring into me.

"Hello, little kitty," he croons. Even his voice is no longer his own. It's smoother now, almost sultry. "I hadn't planned to take over so soon, but he was falling apart."

I tighten my grip on his throat and push him further away from me at the same time. "Who are you?"

"An interested party. Not that you'll ever find out more than that. It's time for Stephen to fulfil his task before he gets sliced up by you."

"I took the tape off him. He doesn't have any weapons. The mayor is safe."

Stephen - well, whoever is talking through him - laughs. "I never planned to hurt the mayor."

He suddenly goes limp, surprising me. I stumble forward, pulled down by his weight, and he takes that opportunity to kick me with his right foot. A piercing pain explodes in my shin. It's not just pain from a normal shoe-against-leg. This is more. Wetness makes my trousers cling to my skin. I'm bleeding.

I let go of Stephen and jump back, inspecting the damage. A short blade is protruding from Stephen's shoe, coated in my blood. The bastard has cut me. Still, the injury can't be deep, not with that size of weapon. It hurts like hell though. Heat travels up my leg, a strange fire that hurts and burns. I gasp when it reaches my pelvis and races down my other leg. I buckle under the pain and collapse to the ground. Invisible fire devours my skin, more and more, until it's spread across my chest and back.

I can't hold a scream back any longer. The pain is too much. I cry out in agony, while at the same time, Stephen starts to laugh.

"You shouldn't have chosen such a public job. It was too easy to find you."

Yes, I regret that now, trust me. I gasp when the pain flows down my arms. The knife falls from my hand, uselessly landing on the office carpet.

"What are you doing to her?!" Lady Lara yells in outrage. "Stop it at once!"

"I have no intentions of doing so," Stephen says lightly. "You will see why in a minute. It will reveal things that I believe you should know."

"Miss Quim, leave the room. Get the guards," Lara orders.

By now, I'm too weak to crane my neck to see what's going on. The pain is all-consuming, eating me up from the inside. It's reached my neck and breathing is getting harder. I think the flesh in my throat is swelling, constricting my airways. If I don't do something, I'm going to suffocate. But I can't even move. There's nothing I can do but endure and hope it will pass.

The door falls shut; I assume the tailor has left us.

"I know what she is," Lady Lara says loudly. "It's why I employed her. You're not going to tell me something I don't know already."

If I didn't already have trouble breathing, I'd gasp in surprise. How the hell does she know?

"Then perhaps I should kill you too, mayor," Stephen says, his voice cold. "I believed you were innocent in all this. If it turns out that you are secretly supporting *them*, I might have to take action."

"Them?" Lara asks sharply.

"So you don't know. Or do you? No matter, I will know in about a minute."

What the fuck is he talking about? Unless...

Sometimes, back at the Pack, they hurt one of us so much that our bodies shifted involuntarily. It doesn't happen to everyone, but for some, it's an inbuilt defence mechanism. It never happened to me, not even during my close encounters with death and pain, but it sounds like this might be what he's waiting for. He's going to be disappointed. I only shift when I want to and I'm certainly not going to give him the satisfaction.

Someone rips off my fingernails. At least it feels that way. I scream and curl up into a semblance of a ball, but every move hurts. I'm supposed to be the guard, the protector, yet here I am, on the ground, writhing in pain, while the woman I'm employed to protect is standing watch over me. At least that's what I hope she's doing. She's behind me and I don't have the strength to turn around and see what she's up to.

"Is it some kind of poison?" she asks.

It is, I want to reply, but I can barely breathe, let alone speak. Every breath hurts more than the one before.

"Of course. It would have no effect on you though. It only works on a special kind of...people."

"Shifters, you mean."

Damn. She really does know.

"I'm surprised," the man - I no longer want to call him Stephen, since he's definitely someone else now - says in his melodic voice. I bet he's a siren. He must be a powerful one though to control Stephen from a distance. The assistant said that he's getting paid to do it, though, so maybe it's easier to control someone if your victims have a little incentive themselves to follow orders.

"You'd be surprised about a lot of things," Lady Lara replies coolly. "For example, did you know that I recently had some new security installed? Very, very special security technology. It took me a long time to find someone capable of producing it. I had to get someone all the way from the capital, but it was worth it."

As much as I want to cheer her on, I'm starting to lose my hold on consciousness. My brain isn't getting enough oxygen. My body is going into hibernation, followed by death if nothing happens to stop this poison. I always have some antidotes with me, but I've never come across whatever I've been given. All I can hope for is a miracle.

Or, as it turns out, a very clever mayor.

CHAPTER FIFTEEN

Just before I'm fully swallowed by the darkness gnawing on the edges of my mind, a soft humming noise reaches my ears. I doubt it's loud enough for the mayor to hear it. I want to warn her of whatever the siren has planned next, but it takes all the energy I have left to stay conscious. I'm so far gone that I barely even feel the pain.

"That's better," Lady Lara mutters, her voice coming from far away. "Tell me, Stephen, where do you have the antidote? I know even you wouldn't be stupid enough to carry poison without an antidote."

"I-" he stammers, back to his old self.

What's happened to the siren controlling him? Is he gone?

I hear Lara pick up my knife from the floor. I imagine her holding it to Stephen's throat, or maybe his crotch.

"Tell me," she hisses, no longer pretending to be calm. "Now."

"A patch on the back of my neck," he whimpers. He's in pain; she must have cut him. "He said the poison wouldn't hurt me, but it might make me a little sick if I accidentally got in contact with it, so he put a patch on my skin."

"Pray to whatever deity you believe in that there's enough antidote left in the patch," the mayor snaps.

I want to smile. She's one kick-arse woman. She may hide behind her politician persona, but deep inside, she's a fighter who's not afraid to take whatever steps are necessary.

Darkness rolls over me. I hope she cut off his cock.

THE PAIN IN MY LEG IS THE FIRST SENSATION BRUSHING over my tired mind. Next is the strong feeling of being safe. It's something I don't feel very often. When I'm at home with my guys, then yes, but until I met them, until I got free of the Pack, I never ever felt safe.

"Are you awake?"

Her deep, soft voice washes over me like a healing salve.

I groan in response.

"I know you must be in pain, but that's better than you being dead. Right? Think positive. That's my motto. No matter how hard things get. Always remember that the sun rises every morning, even if the night might seem to last forever."

I'd much rather have her give me some painkillers than pretty metaphors.

"I've sent for Bethany," she continues. "The patch seems to have brought you back from the brink, but I doubt it will fully restore you. It was made for humans, after all."

I open my eyes. It takes as much energy as it would usually cost me to climb a house.

"How?" I croak. My voice is barely audible. My throat still feels like it's coated in acid.

"How did I manage to expel the siren?"

I nod weakly.

"I found out about the sirens years ago. It was then that I decided to go into politics. I knew they were running the show and I wanted to give us, normal humans, a chance of governing ourselves. Of course, I've always faked ignorance, no matter how often they tried to make me reveal my knowledge. When I was made mayor, I had someone fit this office with anti-siren technology. Don't ask me how it works because I haven't got a clue." She laughs, a soft sound that dispels some of my pain. "I'm rather glad I invested all that money and effort into it. To be honest, I wasn't even sure if it would work, since it's a prototype."

Once I'm better, I'm going to ask her for the contact details of whoever gave her the technology. I need it, too. Whoever tried to kill me will attempt it again. Today, tomorrow, soon. It's only a matter of time. But I'm no longer going to be taken unprepared. I didn't expect anyone to hunt me here, in Attenburgh, far away from the Pack. Being in the company of the mayor, I never once thought I'd be the target. Even in retrospective, I don't think I would have done anything differently. I got hurt because I tried to protect Lady Lara, and that's my job.

"In case you're wondering about Stephen, he's dead," she says, pulling me from my thoughts. "I had to make it quick because I needed to get help for you. There wasn't time to tie him up until backup arrived. Not that I wanted to do that." Her eyes blaze with anger. "He brought violence into my inner sanctum. This office is supposed to be one of peace. I serve the people of this town, I try to protect them, make their lives better. Every second I spend in here is to help others. His twisted actions have destroyed that."

"How?"

"How did I kill him?"

I nod.

"Thought you'd like to know that. I bet you also want to know if he's still got all his parts attached."

I nod again.

She grins devilishly. "I used your knife, stabbed it in his chest. I think the siren thing left him weak and disoriented; he never even tried to fight back. I pulled out the blade and then stabbed him in the groin. To be honest, seeing and touching his dick didn't seem very appealing, especially not with you dying in the background. Besides, I'm not really interested in dicks."

It takes a moment for my mind to realise what she means. She's gay.

Footsteps in the distance make me turn my head. Bad idea. The world shifts and turns, making my head spin. I close my eyes with a groan.

"Someone's....coming," I wheeze. I barely understand my own words, but Lady Lara seems to get the message. She gets up and grabs my knife. She's cleaned the blade, but I can smell Stephen's blood on it.

I don't even try to sit up. I'm far too weak and it would only result in me using the last energy reserves I have left. I just have to hope that Lady Lara can defend us both, should it be necessary. Some fine bodyguard I am.

Bethany's scent reaches my nose moments before the door bangs open. She runs into the room, her eyes wild as her gaze sweeps over me.

"What the fuck have you done now?"

I roll my eyes - about the most eloquent answer I can give in my current state.

Bethany kneels by my side and takes my pulse.

"What happened?" she asks Lady Lara. The mayor closes the door and takes her seat by my side again. I don't know why she sits on the floor when she could just as well take a seat on her nice leather chair. The one I still envy. It's not like her being close to me is helping with the poison running through my veins.

Lara gives Bethany a quick summary. My friend nods, all professional, and pulls the antidote patch from my neck, taking a few hundred tiny hairs in the process. If I could punch her, I would.

"Oops," she mutters with a grin. She holds up the patch and inspects it closely. It's the first time I get to see it too. It's a black square about an inch wide, looking a bit like a plaster, except for the colour.

"Interesting, that's a great way of administering an antidote," Bethany says appreciatively. "I imagine it would work well for poisons too, although it might be hard to hide it from the target. Still, something to keep in mind."

I bet she's going to start experiments as soon as we get home.

"Kat, do you know what poison you were given?"

I shake my head. I wish I knew.

"That means it's something rare. You were in a lot of pain; were there any other symptoms?"

"Burning," I groan. "Breathing. Hard."

I wish my throat would stop feeling like it's about to walk away from my body.

Bethany frowns. "I can give you something for the symptoms. Lots of painkillers, plus some generic antidotes. That should keep you going until I can analyse your blood in my lab and conjure up something more specific."

"How long will that take?" Lady Lara asks, concern lacing her voice.

How sweet. Is she worried about me? I wonder if that's on a personal or professional level. If I'm out of action, she'll have to look for a new bodyguard. Luckily, I have the guys who'll be able to take turns guarding her. She's proven that she can handle herself, but it's my job to make sure she's safe, and a little poisoning won't stop me in taking that seriously.

"You don't look like you can swallow much, so I'll give you an injection," Bethany explains moments before a needle sinks into my arm. It's a sign of how weak I am that I don't instinctively fight back.

"You may feel a little woozy; I've given you quite a strong dose. Now we better get you home. Mayor, can you organise some transport?"

Woozy? I feel great. I'm floating on rainbows, I'm riding unicorns, I fly on the back of perytons. This is better than catnip, and that says a lot. I leave the humans to it and simply enjoy the ride.

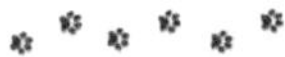

BY THE TIME WE ARRIVE AT HOME, THE UNICORNS HAVE disappeared and new pain has taken their place. Or maybe it's old pain. I no longer care. All I know is that my entire body hurts and that my throat has started to constrict again.

"What the fuck happened to her?"

Lennox and Gryphon crowd me, their concerned faces popping in and out of my field of vision. Without rainbows, the world looks disappointingly bleak.

"Poison," Bethany explains. "But I don't know which one. A siren gave it to her. Well, not the siren himself; he controlled a human who administered it through a spike in his boot. She almost died, but luckily, the human had an antidote patch on him. It's stopped working though. She's deteriorating."

I'm right here, don't talk to me like I'm not there.

Sadly, I can't speak with the way my throat is swelling up. Breathing hurts. I hate feeling so out of control, so weak, so helpless. I'm going to kill the siren who put me in this situation. He's going to suffer until he's a trembling mess on the floor.

"A siren?" Gryphon asks, a frown appearing on his scarred face. "Kat, did the poison have a particular smell?"

I manage to shake my head. It's not like I sniffed the human's boot, but I didn't smell anything as far as I remember.

"That narrows it down a lot. Definitely no scent of roses?"

I'm poisoned, not stupid. I shake my head.

"Alright. Bethany, I'll join you in the lab. I'll make some antidotes to the most common siren poisons, starting with the most likely ones. But first, I think you could do with some more painkillers, Kat."

Damn right.

He gently strokes my cheek, a gesture so soft that I quiver beneath his touch. I hate him when he walks away from me to get his medical kit.

Luckily, Lennox is still there, taking Gryphon's place.

"Does it hurt a lot?" he asks, his voice hoarse with concern.

I want to shake my head to reassure him, but my body betrays me. A new wave of pain races through me and tears stream from my eyes.

"Oh kitty cat, I'm so sorry," Lennox whispers. "I wish there was something I could do."

He takes my hand and squeezes it. I grip it tightly when the next tsunami of agony crashes over me. I don't know if I can stand this for much longer. The pain is all-encompassing, reaching from my toes to my scalp. It's going to be hard to make the siren feel this much pain as retribution. A challenge for my torture skills.

"Kat, do you know who did this? Did you recognise the siren?"

I shake my head. How could I? I don't know any sirens in Attenburgh – with the exception of Gryphon, obviously, who we kind of imported.

Just when I think of him, he returns with his medical kit.

"Shall I put you to sleep?" he asks. "I don't think any of my analgesics will be strong enough to completely take the pain away."

I shake my head. I don't want to be out of commission. What if the siren returns? Well, I wouldn't be able to do anything. I can't even lift my head. I sigh and nod. A nap sounds good.

Lennox kisses my forehead. "When you wake up, everything will be okay again."

You better keep your promise. I don't feel like dying.

CHAPTER SIXTEEN

I wake up without pain. I flex my hands, roll my head from side to side. No pain. Thank the great fluffy cat in the heavens.

"Hey, sis."

I blink open my eyes and look at myself. No, it's Caitlin. I blink again, trying to get rid of my slightly blurry vision. The world still looks hazy. I wipe my eyes and my vision finally clears. Yellow gunk sticks to my fingers. Yuck. That came from my eyes? Weird.

"How are you feeling?" she asks. Unlike with the guys earlier, there's no concern in her voice. That's my sister for you. Strong, composed, feline. I want to compliment her on it, but I'll save that for later. There are more important things to talk about.

"How long did I sleep for?" I ask. Well, I try. My voice sounds like a saw grating against stone.

Caitlin grins and hands me a glass of water. I sit up, again surprised at how easy it feels. I don't have my usual strength and my back is a little stiff, but the pain is completely gone.

I empty the glass in one gulp. The water flushes away the bad taste in my mouth that I hadn't even noticed until it was gone.

"For a while," my sister replies. "I finally managed to persuade your mates to get some sleep and let me keep watch over you. Trust me, it took a lot of persuasion. Even more threats." She grins. "At least now I know what threats work on them. For the future. Next time you're unconscious for days."

"Days?" I ask in trepidation. "What day is it?"

"Friday morning. I'm afraid to say that it was no beauty sleep. You're still as ugly as before."

I growl at her. "You look like me. If I'm ugly, then you're the same."

"Never said I wasn't."

"You need to work on your self-confidence, sis. You're pretty and that means I am too. Now tell me what's been going on while I was out."

"Well, Ryker almost killed Gryphon, then Gryphon almost killed Lennox, and so on. Please don't do this to them again. Those boys completely lose control without you there to hold their leashes."

"Boys? They're older than you."

Caitlin shrugs. "They behaved like teenagers. It didn't take Bethany and Gryphon very long to mix up an antidote, thanks to the patch that they could use as a template, but your body needed time to heal. Yesterday evening, you shifted and everyone thought you were about to wake up, but you just continued to sleep before shifting back a couple of hours ago. It was very weird."

"Do you know what poison the siren gave me?"

She shakes her head. "No, and neither do the others. It's something none of us has come across before. At least now we have an antidote. Beth has made a whole batch of it that us shifters can carry with us from now on."

"I doubt the siren is going to use the same trick again. He'll think of a new way to attack me, but this time, I know he's out there. I'll be on my guard. And so should you. We look similar enough that he might mistake you for me."

"Don't worry, I'm always careful. If it had been me in that room, I would have never let him close."

"And the mayor would probably be dead."

She shrugs. "Better her than me."

"And that's exactly why you're not on the bodyguarding roster." I sit up straight when I realise that today is the big day. "Is the jewellery thing still on?"

"If you mean the heist, yes. If you mean you guarding the mayor, then no. Lennox is doing that instead. He looks the most normal out of all of the guys."

I laugh. "Unless he shifts."

"Yup, unless that."

I have no intention of letting him take my place by Lady Lara's side, but I don't tell her that. Not yet.

"Tell me about your plans for the heist," I ask.

"Benjamin and I are doing the actual diamond stealing. Lily will be there as a guest for backup. She's managed to seduce a guy going there, so she's his plus one. Ryker and his cats will be patrolling the area to find the best escape routes. Beth stays here; she's not really interested in doing the heavy work, although I bet she's going to want a share of the spoils."

"What about Gryphon?"

"He'll be here too, babysitting you, making sure you don't do what I know you're already planning."

I feign innocence. "I'm planning to stay in bed and

sleep. Maybe read a little; I never have time for that usually."

"Yeah, sure. You forget, we're clones. I know you better than you think. Gryphon has permission to bribe you with catnip, so you better behave."

Catnip. My mouth waters. Although to be honest, I don't know if I can appreciate catnip after those rainbow painkillers.

"I almost wish I were in your position. Nobody ever offers me catnip."

"Because we don't know how it would interact with your meds."

Caitlin rolls her eyes. "Yeah, I know, I know. I'm still jealous."

"Back to the heist. What will you do with the diamond afterwards? Give it to the people who told us about it in the first place?"

"We haven't decided yet. I think the guys want to let you make the decision. My idea is that we pretend to want to give it to them, that way we'll find out who's behind it. If they're nice, we can sell it, if they're not, we kill them."

I chuckle. "That's a nice plan. The only problem is that they may be sirens. Did you think of that?"

She shrugs. "It doesn't change anything. Unless one of them is the evil siren who tried to kill you, I don't care if we're dealing with sirens, humans, shifters or aliens, as long as they pay us. I'm not planning to become their friend. It's a business transaction, plain and simple."

"You'd do business with sirens? After all they did to us?"

"Gryphon's a siren and he's one of the good guys. I bet there are other friendly sirens out there, we just have to find them."

I decide not to argue. I need to save my strength for tonight.

"Has anything else happened while I was sleeping? Any news of our sister?"

Her smile disappears. "Nothing. Not a single rumour that would match K7. She's either not in this town, hidden really well or no longer alive."

"Let's focus on the first two. I refuse to assume that we have yet another sister to bury."

Caitlin nods. "Agreed. Once you're better, you might be able to use your position with the mayor to search for her."

"I'd planned that. Has Lady Lara been in touch about my future with her?"

"Yes, she even sent flowers, but the kittens ate them. She expects you to return to work as soon as you're better."

I breathe a sigh of relief. I'd dreaded her firing me. Not just because it would deprive me of her resources to find K7. Also because I like her, for some strange reason. And it's kind of fun to have an actual job.

Caitlin's mention of the kittens makes me think of another animal in this house.

"How's Willow?" I ask.

She grins. "Walking around like she owns this place. She's somehow become the leader of the kittens. Don't ask me how that works; she's supposed to be prey. Benjamin is spoiling her whenever he gets the chance. You might want to have a word with him before the poor deer is as round as a barrel."

I laugh. "I can't wait to see her. But I'm still a little tired; I think I'll have another nap."

Caitlin gives me a suspicious look. "You don't look tired."

"That's because I'm a master of disguise. Now run off so I can get some shut-eye."

She looks like she's about to protest, but I glare at her before yawning loudly. With a last suspicious glance, she leaves me to myself.

As soon as I hear her walking down the stairs, I get up and walk over to the window. A post-it note has been stuck to the glass.

DON'T YOU DARE LEAVE.

I snort. As if that would stop me.

I open the window and find yet another note on the outside window sill.

I'M WARNING YOU.

The handwriting is that of Gryphon. You can see his posh upbringing in the way he elegantly curves his Gs and Ys.

The big question is, how far will he go to stop me from leaving? Will there be anything worse than post-its? In his shoes, I'd put up some traps, maybe some darts laced with sleeping poison. Or some kind of alert that will be triggered as soon as I leave the room. No, I doubt he's that sophisticated; it would be a bit over the top.

Still, I make sure to look for traps all around the window frame, but as I thought, there's nothing. I'm being too paranoid. I pocket the note, as a reminder to take revenge on Gryphon, and jump onto the window sill, crouching low. I'm on the second floor, but the jump won't hurt me. Cats always land on their feet.

A meow from below makes me focus on the kitten looking up at me. It's Teapot, the tabby who specialises in waking me up in the morning. Evil little cat. She stares at me with her bright green eyes, as if she's daring me to jump. Despite the distance, I can read the surface of her thoughts. She's planning to run to Gryphon to report on me. Okay, she's worse than evil. This little kitten might look like pure innocence, but she's delighted at the thought of snitching.

The way down is barred - by a kitten, of all things. That only leaves the roof. The walls of our house are old and have enough crevices between the bricks that make it easy to climb. I've done it before. Question is, what awaits me on the roof? I'm starting to dread that Gryphon has thought of everything.

There's no way I'm staying cooped up inside though, so I start climbing. My muscles protest at the exertion; I've spent too much time in bed. And fighting the poison that tried to kill me.

It takes me way longer than usual to reach the roof. I sit down for a moment, letting my muscles relax. I feel like I've aged by several decades overnight. This is no fun at all. The list of things I'm going to do to the siren is increasing steadily. I'll need several days to fit in all the torture techniques I've got planned for him. He'll beg me for mercy, but I highly doubt I'll give it to him. He watched as I lay on the floor, writhing in pain. I imagine he enjoyed the sight. No, he won't get any mercy from me. His death will be long and extremely painful.

I smile at the thought of hurting the siren. First, though, I have to find him. In a city full of sirens, and without ever having seen his real face, that will be difficult. Stephen's voice changed when the siren spoke through him, but I don't know if that was anywhere close to the siren's actual voice. For now, I'm in the dark about his identity. I need to force him to step out in the open, to confront me directly.

A strange buzzing sound makes me tense up. Is that a - yes, a tiny remote-controlled helicopter comes into view as it rises in a straight line. I always wanted to have one of those as a child, but of course I didn't have the money, nor would I have been allowed to possess one. They would have taken it away as soon as they spotted me with a toy. We weren't even allowed teddy bears. Nothing that could distract us from our purpose: becoming weapons for the Pack. Assassins didn't need stuffed toys.

I make a mental note to send Little Kat a teddy bear. She's still young enough to reclaim her childhood. Maybe Auntie Rose has already given her toys - yes, I bet she has, she's amazing like that - but I want to make sure my baby sister doesn't miss out on anything. Once we've got the diamond, we might be able to return home for a bit to visit her. The official reason will be to sell the jewel, of course. I don't want people to know how precious my siblings are to me. That would make them targets, and after my encounter with the siren's poison, I'm even more determined to avoid that.

The helicopter hovers in front of me, close enough for me to see the message bound to its landing gear.

YOU SHOULD HAVE LISTENED.

I roll my eyes. More empty threats? This is starting to get old.

"Come out and show yourself!" I shout. "If you want to stop me from leaving, try and do so in person."

Gryphon's laughter drifts up to me. He's enjoying this. Well, to be honest, so am I. I'm kind of flattered how much effort he's put into this game.

I snatch the helicopter out of the air, almost cutting myself on the sharp rotor blades. It's mine now. My precious. Gryphon seems to realise that I've caught his toy, because it turns off without warning. I'll have to steal the remote control from him later. Already, I'm making plans of how I could use this helicopter to my advantage. I could load it with explosives. I could have it carry a bag of poison that it could drop onto a target. All the possibilities. One thing is for sure, I'm going to have fun with this.

"Have you decided to stay yet?" Gryphon shouts from below.

"No way!"

"Then I guess I have to come up!"

I can't suppress a grin. Let the hunt begin.

CHAPTER SEVENTEEN

He tackles me as soon as he reaches the roof. I squeal and let him push me down onto my back, pretending I'm all weak and frail.

His smile drops a little, as if he's concerned that he's hurt me. I take that moment of insecurity to flip us over until I'm on top of him. I straddle his body, pinning his legs down with my own, and push his arms above his head, holding a tight grip on his wrists. He doesn't struggle, probably playing the same game I was.

When I've got him exactly where I want him, I hesitate. What now? Usually, I'd cut my mark's throat once I've got them secured, or threaten them until they give me the information I want. Gryphon needs neither killing nor torturing.

"Kiss me," he groans.

Or I could do that.

I grin and adjust my position until my lips are hovering above his. He doesn't wait for me to kiss him; he pushes up despite my hold on him and his lips crash against mine.

I let go of his wrists to cup his face, taking control of

the situation. Whenever he tries to deepen the kiss, I push him down. It's fun to tease him, but after a while, I'm craving more. I let go and he takes full advantage of it. He reaches up and tangles his fingers in my hair.

I moan when his tongue nudges against my own, encouraging me to join him in dance. What starts off as a gentle waltz soon turns into a rhythmic tango, full of passion and energy.

I forget everything around me. I no longer care that we're on a roof. I don't care that he's managed to stop me from leaving. And I certainly don't care that people might be able to see us. It's not like we're naked - not yet, anyway. I rub my body against Gryphon's, trying to satisfy the itch deep within me. Kissing him is amazing, freeing, beautiful, but it's not quite enough. His hardness presses against me, showing me that he feels the same.

"Do we return to your room?" he asks hoarsely, breaking the kiss for just long enough to pose the question, before claiming my mouth once more. He seems to have forgotten that I need to speak to reply.

Oh well, it seems like I don't have any other option. I slide my hands between us and grasp his shirt. It's one of his black button-up shirts that he wears when he's not sneaking about in the night. They're perfect to be ripped open, so that's exactly what I do. The sound of buttons rolling down roof tiles makes me grin devilishly against his lips.

I run my hands over his now exposed chest, exploring the hard planes of his muscles for the umpteenth time. I barely notice his scars anymore; they're not important. We all have them, it's just that his are on the surface while many of us carry them inside.

"I love it when you touch me like that," he whispers. "Don't stop."

"I have no intention of stopping. You're way too yummy not to touch."

He chuckles. "Yummy?"

I nod and lick across his collarbone. "Positively delicious."

His chest shakes with laughter. "You're unique, Kat. Utterly unique."

"I sure hope so. What, with all my clones and that."

"They make you even more unique," he says, this time without laughing. "They may have the same genes, they may look like you, but you're totally different from all of them. You're special, Kat. Kind, clever, ambitious, creative, crazy..."

"I agree with all of those."

"...humble." Gryphon grins. "And in addition to all that, you're also the most amazing woman in the world. If I'd never met you, but knew you existed and how perfect you are, I'd stayed celibate for the rest of my life."

I scoff. "No, you wouldn't have. You're way too horny for that."

To prove a point, I reach between us and put my hand on his crotch. He groans as I squeeze his hard cock through the fabric of his trousers.

"I guess we'll never know. And it doesn't matter. I found you and now you're mine."

I give him another squeeze and he jerks beneath me. "Wrong. You're mine."

Enough words. I don't want to talk. I want to take him, here on this roof, for all the world to see. I'm claiming him, Gryphon, the siren who switched sides, who followed his heart. Who followed me.

I bend down and kiss him, putting all that into the kiss. I hope he'll understand what I'm trying to tell him. I won't be able to say the words. Not yet.

*   *   *

IT TURNS OUT THAT A TILED ROOFTOP IS NOT THE MOST comfortable place. If I weren't a fast-healing shifter, I'd have bruises all over my back. Gryphon groans as we climb through the window and back into my room. Both of us stretch, trying to get rid of the aches.

"It worked," he laughs while arching his back. "You stayed."

"Only for a while. I still don't plan to stay here all day while the rest of M.E.O.W. get to have all the fun. I bet you don't want to sit here either and twiddle your thumbs, right?"

"I could twiddle my thumbs inside your-"

"Don't start," I interrupt him with a glare. "That seduction technique only worked once."

"Seduction? I never did any seduction. That was all you. But if you'd like me to give you a demonstration, maybe mixed in with some siren magic..."

"No, thanks." I actually regret declining his offer of yet more sex. I love it when he uses his magic. It makes everything more intense without feeling out of touch with reality. Not like catnip, which distorts reality. Gryphon's magic just amplifies it.

"What do I have to do to persuade you to stay here with me?" he asks. There's no confidence in his voice. He's just asking this as a formality so he can say he tried to stop me.

"Find me a two-horned unicorn that was born at midnight on a full moon," I counter. "With two tails, one of them green, the other blue. If you can't do that, then I'm afraid you won't be able to keep me in this house, no matter how often you try to get me laid."

"You know, I could always try to tie you up."

I raise an eyebrow. "You wish."

"Yes, I do wish. Maybe another time."

"In your dreams."

Gryphon sighs. "I should have given you something to keep you asleep for longer. Arguing with you is so exhausting."

I point at the bed. "If you're exhausted, go have a lie-down. Don't mind me." I give him an innocent smile. "I'll be downstairs."

"Sure you will." He sighs again. "I guess I tried. And I really don't know where to find a unicorn. Maybe at the Jewellers' Guild party? It seems like a place where such posh creatures would hang out."

"Maybe. I think I should accompany you just to make sure you select the right unicorn."

Our eyes meet and we stare at each other for a few seconds before bursting into laughter. I love how easy it is to spend time with Gryphon. There are no awkward silences, no misunderstandings. We have the same quirky sense of humour and our thoughts seem strangely aligned. It's strange how perfect he is for me even though he's not a cat, not even a shifter.

I start sifting through my wardrobe, looking for the perfect outfit for tonight. Luckily, I won't have to wear that dress after all. If Miss Quim ever actually made it. After what her assistant did, after me being unconscious for days, she probably thought I wouldn't need it. Which I don't.

"What's the plan?" Gryphon asks. "I'm assuming you have one?"

"The plan is to steal the diamond without being detected by either the guards nor my team. Then to get out without being caught. No dying, either. Simple, right?"

A moment of silence is followed by Gryphon's wild laughter. "You want to work against the others?"

"Why not? It's a good exercise. The two of us against the rest of M.E.O.W. It's the perfect test to see who's best."

He groans. "Lily is going to kill me. She was very particular about you staying in bed and resting."

"Lily is way too emotional. She gets overly cautious when people she likes are involved. It's why she has a hard time making friends." I freeze. Oops. I shouldn't have said that. My tongue was faster than my brain.

Luckily, Gryphon doesn't comment on me psychoanalysing my best friend.

"Are you sure we can do this? Don't get me wrong, we're the best assassins in this town, maybe in the country, but the others have a clear advantage. Caitlin has planned the heist for days. Benjamin has scouted out the venue and knows all the ways in and out. Lily will be in the crowd, close enough to see how well-guarded the diamond is and how to go about stealing it. And even if we had the same knowledge as them, how are we supposed to get past the cats? Ryker has them patrolling the area. There's no way we can evade their attention."

He's right about the last bit. The cats would rat us out to Ryker without hesitation. They like me, they respect me, but he's their family. Even intimidation won't get me their obedience.

I pull my leather jumpsuit from the wardrobe - there wasn't really any other choice - while racking my brain for a way to make the heist work.

"Catnip," I mutter thoughtfully. "How about we drug them?"

"Did you just suggest drugging cats?"

"Since nobody is letting me have my catnip, I'm just being nice and want to share it with the rest of Attenburgh's feline population," I say with an innocent smile. "I think they call it being a philanthropist. *Felin*trophist."

"You think you're so clever," he mocks with a loving smile.

"I am. Do you know where Lily has hidden the catnip?"

"As a matter of fact, I do. But I'm not convinced yet that I should tell you. Kat, this plan is rubbish. We might have a chance against the others, but not against the cats."

"Are you admitting to cats being generally superior to all other life on Earth?"

"No," he says immediately. "Just in this case. There's more of them. Can't you influence them somehow? Hypnotise them?"

"That's your area of expertise. Maybe you should sing them all to sleep."

"If we knock them out, we can't rely on their help either. No, we need to get them on our side."

I sigh. "I don't know how to do that. I'm not very good at telling people what to do. Well, I'm good at telling them, they're just not very good at actually doing what I say."

"You're kidding, right?"

I frown at him. "I'm not."

"Kat, you're deluded. You inspire people all the time. Who do you think is holding M.E.O.W. together? You took a group of loners and misfits and turned them into a team. We might not always do what you say, but we'd follow you into the pits of hell if necessary. And if it's life and death, of course we'd follow your commands." He grins. "Unless we know better. Then we'd let you know."

I'm not quite sure what to say to that, so I stay silent. It doesn't matter anyway. I need to find a way to deal with the cats, not bathe in Gryphon's compliments.

"What if we turn it into a competition for the cats as

well?" I suggest after a while. "Turn them into two teams. Cats are even more competitive than humans. They'll love the chance to prove themselves. Half of them can work for Ryker, the other half for me. A prize will be offered to whatever feline team wins, even if it's not mine. And as part of the deal, they won't let Ryker know that you and I are trying our own heist."

"That could work. I assume the prize will be catnip?"

I grin. "Obviously."

CHAPTER EIGHTEEN

I lie down again, pretending to be ill and tired, until everyone but Beth and Gryphon has left the house. Both Lennox and Ryker are adorable, asking me if it's okay if they leave and let me on my own. I reassure them that I'll be sleeping most of the day and that Gryphon will be here if I need anything. I feel a little bad about deceiving them, but they've all been very clear about not allowing me to go with them. Lennox made threats of tying me to the bed as soon as I mentioned it.

Beth has retreated to the outhouse, her arms full of snacks. She's going to enjoy not having to share them with the rest of the team. I don't mind she's sacked our pantry. It will keep her occupied and distracted.

As soon as everyone's gone, I jump out of bed, put on my jumpsuit and swing my weapons belt around my waist. The leather suit has inbuilt calf and arm sheaths for my knives. I fill them all with blades. You can never be too prepared. If the siren resurfaces, I need to be able to defend myself.

I open my box of poison darts, glad Bethany has found

time to refill them. Usually, I prefer the deadly ones, but today I take mostly sleep darts. This isn't an assassination, it's a heist. I don't want to kill the guards, just stop them from catching me. I'm sure they deserve a nap after all that guarding, right?

I join Gryphon in the living room. He's suited up as well, carrying just as many weapons as myself. He points to a bulge on his chest.

"Smoke bombs. Just in case we need a distraction."

"Did you make them?"

"Benjamin did. He made them for Caitlin, but I managed to steal some."

I laugh. "You stole from a thief? Well done you."

"He was busy fawning over his fawn. He didn't even want to take part in the heist until Bethany promised to keep an eye on the little deer. He's completely obsessed with it."

"That's Benjamin for you. He loves his animals."

"Speaking of animals, are there any cats around?"

I extend my senses and find one cat sleeping in one of the empty bedrooms. I think I recognise the scent, but we have so many cats running around the house that it's getting hard to keep them apart. There are eight kittens in Benjamin's room too, but for what we're planning, we need a grown-up cat.

I whistle sharply and hear the cat meow in response.

"One cat, should be here in a moment. Are you all ready to go?"

Gryphon nods. "Let's do this. Even if the others win, it's great to get to spend more time with you. Just the two of us."

I smile at him. "I agree. We need to do this more often. Minus the poisoning and me almost dying."

"Does that mean you're open to more roof sex?"

I groan and stretch my back at the memory of the uncomfortable tiles. "Maybe not, unless you bring a mattress."

A meow keeps him from answering. James strolls into the room, his tail straight in the air as always. Sometimes I wonder if he can't curl up his tail or if he thinks he's prettier or more intimidating this way. He's a small but feral looking Bengal cat with round brown splotches on his back and delicate stripes around his neck. He's one of the cats who came with us when we moved to Attenburgh.

"Hey James."

He rubs against my legs and I rub his head in response. He purrs, making his tail vibrate. I laugh at the sight. He once led me to the Pack headquarters, the day Gryphon and I killed their leaders. I think James will be on my side. I hope so, anyway.

"Did they leave you behind?"

He sends me a mental image of him sitting on my chest, preventing me from getting up.

I snicker. "You're my guard cat?"

He purrs in confirmation.

"How would you like to earn yourself some catnip?"

His ears twitch. Now I've got his attention.

I explain the plan to him, checking from time to time that he understands. Cats are clever, but sometimes things get lost in translation. When I'm done, he sends me an image of himself rolling around with a ball of string, his eyes glazed in catnip stupor.

I grin and turn to Gryphon. "He's on our side."

"Brilliant. We better go now or the others might steal the diamond before we even get there."

"James, you run ahead and inform the other cats. Tell the ones in our team to wait for us near the venue so we can see which ones are on our side. And be sure to instruct them all not to breathe a single word to Ryker. This is a secret. Whoever blabs to him will never get a single crumb of catnip from me ever again."

The cat inclines his head and runs off with one last shake of his straight tail.

I exchange a look with Gryphon. "Ready to go on a diamond heist?"

He shoots me a wide smile. "After you, my lady."

THE VENUE IS A GROUP OF INTERCONNECTED PAVILIONS IN the Botanic Garden. It's the first time I've come here. I don't really see the point of having a garden in the middle of town that you have to pay to enter, when you could just run through the forests and fields outside the city. Humans are weird.

Colourful paper lanterns decorate the trees in the park, and a long row of candles illuminate the way to the Jewellers' Guild ball. A few latecomers hurriedly walk towards the pavilions, but Gryphon and I keep to the shadows, away from the official path. The smell of dozens of cats is a constant reminder that we're being watched. I hope they've agreed to our plan. We'll find out as soon as we meet James. I take a deep breath and search for his scent.

"He's close," I whisper.

We move through the darkness, me leading the way, Gryphon close behind me. He told me once that his senses are a bit better than that of an ordinary human, but his night vision is quite poor. I try to lead us along a route without any roots or other trip hazards. If he ends up with a twisted ankle, this heist will be over before it's even begun.

James waits for us in between two ancient oak trees about two hundred yards away from the pavilions. A cacophony of voices and music drifts towards us and I have to put some effort into filtering out the noise so that I can focus on my immediate surroundings.

The Bengal cat has assembled thirteen cats. My favourite number. I'm tempted to give him a praising head rub, but I don't want to undermine his authority amongst his group. Cuddles can be done after we've got the diamond.

"Well done," I whisper. "You all know what to do? You're not allowed to talk to Ryker or Caitlin, or use any other means of communication to let them know Gryphon and I are here."

All fourteen cats send me their mental affirmation. Some are keener than others, but I believe none of them will betray us. Cats may be fiercely independent and headstrong, but they do adhere to an honour code of sorts. Like peeing only on freshly washed clothes, or lying exactly where a human wants to sit.

"I need you to patrol the area," I tell them, making sure to look at each of them at least once to build a connection. "Gryphon and I may have to leave very quickly and we'll need an escape route where we won't get seen by humans. I also want you to have our backs. If you see a threat, someone sneaking up on us, or, worse, the rest of M.E.O.W. realising that we're here, you have to warn me right away. Understood?"

They all bow their heads. Ryker taught them that this is how humans signal their agreement.

"Good. Have any of you come close enough to the event to see the diamond?"

A wave of confusion rams into me. Ouch. Fourteen confused cats is not a nice sensation on a telepathic level.

"A diamond is a shiny stone," I explain. "As if someone's taken a star from the sky and has put it into a rock."

"Very poetic," Gryphon whispers. "What's next, *Poetry for Cats* by bestselling author Katriona Feln?"

I elbow him, aiming for his ribs but only grazing his flat stomach. Despite the darkness, he's fast.

"Does everyone understand?" I ask once again.

This time, all I get is impatience. I grin. Those cats are just as ready to earn some catnip than I am.

"James, you're with us," I mutter. "We might need one of you for a distraction."

The Bengal rubs against my leg. Such a cutie. But now's not the time to think of how lovely it would be to have him on my lap and stroke his head, scratching behind his ears. No, it's time to steal a big star rock.

CHAPTER NINETEEN

The security is tight around the pavilions. They didn't control entrance to the park; I guess they're not allowed to do that since it's town property, but a guard is posted every few metres around the venue. They all wear the same unflattering uniform that makes them look fat and sluggish. Probably on purpose, to deceive any attacker, unless this is the worst group of security guards in history. They have a variety of weapons with them, ranging from knives to sabres to crossbows. None of them has a firm grip on their weapons though, signalling that they don't expect a threat right now. They'll probably assume they're just here as a formality.

"James, we need to find out in which pavilion the diamond is being kept," I whisper while observing the guards. "And do you know where the others are at the moment?"

He sends me an image of Lily on the arm of an elderly gentleman. She wears a pink ball gown that I've never seen before. It suits her body, but it certainly doesn't suit her personality. Next is a vision of Ryker crouching on a roof. I can't quite make out which pavilion he's on. There's four of them, connected by roofed pathways, their wooden columns covered in ivy. Large rose bushes hide whatever's in the middle of the buildings, but judging from the sound of gurgling water, there has to be a stream nearby. I imagine a pond with overweight koi carp and a bored duck or two. It would fit well into this garden.

"What about the others?" I ask James.

He shakes his head. That's all he knows.

"Alright, I'm sure your cats will be able to give us an update soon. I guess until then, we're doing this the old-fashioned way."

"I love being old-fashioned," Gryphon jokes. "May I assist you, milady? Could I hold this door open for you? Would you need help with unzipping your dress?"

"I'll assist you in dying if you don't stop this," I hiss back. "Do we split up or go together?"

"Usually, I'd suggest splitting up, but that doubles the chance of one of the others spotting us. I'm way more wary of them than of those guards."

"Same. Let's start with the pavilion on our right. It smells nice."

It must be where the buffet is located. A myriad of alluring scents drifts on the wind from that direction. Grilled chicken, caramelised goat cheese, crispy bacon, scrumptious chocolate pudding.

"We should have had dinner," Gryphon whispers as we stalk towards the food pavilion. "This is making my stomach grumble."

"Why do you think we're going there? I doubt the diamond is hidden among the chicken."

He laughs. "You're so greedy. And a very bad thief. We shouldn't get distracted by food."

"No, we really shouldn't," I agree. "But since it's there...I bet they have far too much. They'd end up throwing perfectly good food away and that would be bad from an ethical perspective. We'd be helping them by stealing a plateful or two."

"I completely agree with your logic. Roof? Distraction for the guards?"

I turn to him and grin. "I think you haven't used your siren skills in a while. We can't let them get all rusty, can we."

Gryphon rolls his eyes. "Only because I'm hungry too."

We sneak as close as we can without leaving the cover of the bushes. I'm grateful to whoever planted these thornless, thick-leaved bushes. They're perfect to hide behind.

Once we're in position, Gryphon purses his lips and whistles softly. It's nothing like the sharp whistle I use to call a cat to me. No, this is music wrapped into a single note, eliciting emotions and thoughts it shouldn't be able to. I focus on my mental defences, strengthening them. I'm not as susceptible to Gryphon's magic as humans, but it can be distracting.

Two of the guards leave their posts and walk towards us. Their expressions are blank, their eyes unfocused. Gryphon has them under his spell.

When they reach us, he quickly reaches up to touch each of them. It will strengthen his power over them, or so he once told me.

His whistling song changes, becoming quieter, yet it fills me with a strange sense of urgency. The guards must feel the same, but amplified. They turn and rush back to the pavilion.

"I've told them to get us a selection of everything," Gryphon says, interrupting his magic music.

"Great. Are we turning this heist into a picnic?"

He shrugs. "All the best adventures are accompanied by an epic meal."

"Are they?"

"From now on, they are. Let's let the cats do some of the leg work while we relax a little. Remember, you need to recover your strength."

As much as I want to protest, he's right.

"Food will be great for that," I joke, unwilling to openly admit that it's true. I'm not quite back to normal. I'm healing, I can almost feel my broken cells knitting themselves back together, but it'll take some time until I'm all back to normal. Whatever that poison was, I don't want to ever get in contact with it again.

We sit down on the grass while we wait for the guards to return. James lies down a few yards away from us. I wish I could imagine that it was just the two of us here, but there are way too many sounds and smells that keep distracting me. I let my mind drift, honing in on some of the conversations happening in the pavilions.

"...have you tried the wine? It's been aged in black oak barrels..."

"...my arthritis is particularly bad today..."

"...wonder how Kat is doing."

I tense up and focus on the voices. It's hard to consciously focus on one particular conversation, but it helps that I know who's talking. Lady Lara, the mayor of Attenburgh.

"She's recovering well," Lennox replies. "She would have loved to accompany you today, but she wasn't quite up to it yet."

I growl. He makes me sound like an invalid.

"What is it?" Gryphon asks, but I shush him with a wave of my hand.

"You can tell her that she'll be able to wear the beautiful dress Miss Quim made her at a future occasion," Lara continues, her voice dripping with sarcasm. She knows exactly how much I'll hate that.

"I'm sure she'll be delighted," Lennox replies with just as much mirth.

I want to throw something at them. Making fun of me like that is not nice, but exactly what I expected. And what I would have done in their shoes.

"Have you seen the diamond yet?" Lennox asks innocently. "I've been told it's quite spectacular."

"Who told you about the diamond?"

I can almost see Lady Lara raise her perfect eyebrows.

"I can't reveal my sources," Lennox hedges. "But of course we had to do some enquiries to make sure we can protect you as best as possible. That includes potential thieves who might be after the most valuable item at this event."

"Lower your voice," Lara whispers. "It's supposed to be a surprise. The diamond will be revealed at the end of the night as a symbol of what the guild can achieve when everyone works together. Last I heard, they were planning to split it up between every member of the guild."

I gasp in surprise. Gryphon shoots me a questioning look but I can't explain it to him just now, I need to concentrate on eavesdropping.

Lennox seems just as perplexed. "Wait, they're going to destroy the diamond?"

"Yes. It's far too valuable to keep it locked up somewhere. No matter how good the security, someone would always try to steal it. By breaking it into smaller parts, everyone gets to share in the wealth. But not everyone agreed with that plan, so I'm not sure if it's been officially decided or not."

Gryphon's whistle breaks my concentration. The two guards have returned, each carrying a serving tray laden with food. They've done well. My mouth waters at the sight of chilli-coated drumsticks. I snatch one from the plate before the guard has even set down the tray on the grass.

"You may return to your posts now," Gryphon says in a gentle, melodic tone. "You will not remember any of this. Should you see us later, you will ignore us."

The guards bow their heads and turn, walking away without another look. I know he did this little scene for my benefit. He could have given his orders through his magic alone, but he probably wants some recognition.

"Nicely done," I say with a smile. "Now let's eat."

I grab two of the drum sticks - one for each hand - and start ripping the juicy meat off the bone. Delicious.

"What did you find out? You were listening for quite a while." Gryphon takes his time choosing what he wants to eat. By the time he'll start, I'll already be done with my drumsticks.

"Lara and Lennox," I explain between bites."

"Lara? You're calling her Lara now?"

I shrug. "She offered. I think she dislikes formality just as much as I do."

He looks sceptical, but doesn't stay with the topic. He pops a grape in his mouth.

I can't help but laugh.

"What?"

"We have all this amazing food here and you take a grape? You can have that any day of the week."

"I like grapes," he says defensively. "Besides, I know better than to take any of the food you like."

"I'm not that bad."

"Yes, you are. You're insatiable." He grins at me. "In more ways than one."

"Stop the innuendos and eat," I command. "We've got time. They won't reveal the diamond until the end of the event."

I give him a summary of what I heard Lara and Lennox talk about. Gryphon is just as shocked as I was at the plan to destroy the diamond. Well, I guess they're not going to destroy it as such, but it feels like a weird thing to do.

"That must be why someone wants it stolen," I say when I'm done. "It might not be for money at all; they might just want to prevent it from being chopped into pieces."

"Which would mean that the person sponsoring the heist is part of the Jewellers' Guild."

"Exactly. Or someone who knows their inside workings well. It could be a relative of one of the members, or an employee."

"I doubt that," Gryphon muses. "That employee would have to be extremely rich to afford to buy the diamond off us. Maybe we should find out who the richest member of the guild is."

I nod. "Once we've got the diamond, we can do some research. But we have to steal it first, preferably before the others do."

I look around for James. He's no longer where he lay earlier; he must have left while I was busy eavesdropping on conversations. I extend my senses and quickly find his scent. He's not far, and surrounded by the sounds of other cats. They must be providing him with the intel they collected. Once again, I mentally pat myself on the shoulder for recruiting cats to my cause. They're the most efficient spies ever. No human will ever reach their level of subterfuge and cunning.

I eat some more food while waiting for James to return. The chocolate-covered pomegranate seeds are particularly delicious. I could eat them all, but I graciously leave some for Gryphon. He's stuck to grapes for some weird reason, while I've decimated most of the meat dishes. I rarely get food this good. Sending Caitlin to learn how to cook is rising ever higher on my list of priorities. Those drumsticks were to die for, so I bet she'd be great at making them.

In the distance, the music stops and the noise level lowers.

"What are they doing?" Gryphon asks me.

I focus on the sounds drifting from the pavilions. "Speeches. Poor Lennox, he'll have to listen to them all with the mayor."

I'm rather glad I'm not with Lady Lara just now.

James meows to get my attention. The other cats have left and he has rejoined us. His tail is as stiff as a stick as he looks up at me expectantly.

I realise I'm holding a fried sausage in my hand. With a sigh, I hand it to him. I guess he's earned a reward in addition to the promised catnip.

He swallows the sausage in one big gulp and immediately looks around for more.

"Sorry, that was the last one," I say with a chuckle. "I ate all the others."

He glares at me as if I committed a crime.

"Hey, you'll get catnip later, so don't complain. What did the other cats tell you?"

A flurry of images appears in my mind, too fast to make sense of them.

"Slow down," I admonish him. "You know it doesn't work that way."

He gives me a look that would match a human eye roll, then starts again, slower this time, until I've more or less understood what he's trying to tell me.

When he's done, I give him a little tickle behind the ears.

"Good work. Gryphon, it's time to steal a diamond."

CHAPTER TWENTY

I t's only a matter of time until the others spot us. James has shown me several instances of cats having to be persuaded not to tell Ryker about us. For now, the cats are being controlled by their desire for catnip. I doubt they'd go against a direct command of his, so we need to make sure he stays in the dark. Lennox and Lily will be the easiest to evade since they're both within the crowd. Caitlin is sneaking around the pavilion furthest from us and she looks like she's going to be there for a while. Only one cat has spotted Benjamin, however, and that was several minutes ago. He'll have moved on by now.

Benjamin is an amazing thief because he can hide in plain sight. He looks ordinary, plain and boring. Nobody would ever give him a second look unless he draws attention to himself. Which he doesn't. At night, he turns into a shadow, quick and incredibly hard to catch. I sometimes wonder if he's really a hundred per cent human.

"Benjamin was breaking into one of the pavilions through a back door," I tell Gryphon, going over the image

James showed me. "It looked like it's only used for deliveries. Annoyingly, these buildings all look the same, so I have no idea which one he sneaked into."

"It doesn't matter, we should use the fact that everyone's distracted by those speeches. Did the cats show you which pavilion is the least guarded?"

I nod. "That's exactly where we're going."

I lead him away from the food pavilion, staying behind the bushes to hide from the guards. The connecting pathway between the food pavilion and the one on its right is decorated with rose-covered arches. Pretty, but also unnecessary.

Only a few guests mull around here. They're the rebels who don't want to listen to the speeches. I immediately feel a kinship with them, until I take in their posh clothes and accents. Maybe not. Two of them, a man and a woman, step outside the pavilion and stop in the middle of the rose walkway.

"I love you so much," the woman says loudly.

"I'm going to make love to you, right here, right now," the man replies just as theatrically.

I cringe. I don't need to see that.

"Wait," Gryphon whispers as I turn away from the couple. "I think there's more to it."

"You want to watch them have sex?"

"No, I want to see what they're doing while they're pretending to have sex. They loudly announced their intentions to make sure everybody would look away in embarrassment."

Well, that clearly worked on me. We wait in the shadows, watching the couple. They stand close to each other, but they're not kissing nor doing anything else. Gryphon was right. This was just an act.

"I know where it is," the woman whispers so quietly

that Gryphon won't be able to hear it. Even I have to strain my cat senses to make out her words.

"Tell me," the man mutters. His voice has turned cold, almost threatening.

"D- do you have my payment?" She sounds like she's scared of him. This is getting more and more interesting.

"You will get it once you've fulfilled your side of our bargain," the man snarls. "Now where is the diamond?"

I suck in a breath. "They're after the diamond as well," I whisper to Gryphon. "I wonder if they're following the same instructions we did or if they're independent of that."

"In the pond," the woman replies hesitantly. "There is a platform in the pond that will be raised to reveal the diamond to the crowd. That way, it's safe from anyone who might try to get too close to it."

"In the pond," the man repeated. "That's clever. Will you be able to get it?"

"Sir, you only asked me to provide you with the location," she stutters.

"And now I'm asking you to fetch me the diamond. You wouldn't want to disappoint me, would you?"

"N- no. It's just, I can't swim."

Without warning, he grips her by the shoulders and presses her against one of the archways. She cries out in pain as thorns pierce her skin.

"You better do what you're told," he hisses. "You know what happens to people who don't follow my orders."

"Yes, sir," the woman whimpers. "I will get it for you."

"Good. Now run off and do your job while I make sure I'm seen at the speeches. I have a reputation to uphold."

She hurries away, rubbing her arms where he'd grabbed her. I feel a little pity for her. She got herself involved in something bigger than she'd likely anticipated.

"The diamond is in the pond," I tell Gryphon while we

watch the man walk away. "It seems like one of us may have to get wet."

He laughs. "And I assume you don't mean yourself."

"I'm a cat. We're not good with water. You're a siren. You love water. See, easy decision."

"Sirens haven't lived in the sea for about a hundred generations. You know that. I tell you every time you make me do something water-related."

I shrug. "I'm sure the love for the ocean is still in your genes somewhere. Come on, let's go to the pond before the woman drowns herself."

Luck is on our side. The guards who were stationed around this part of the pavilion are still keeping their distance, probably unaware that the couple is no longer having wild sex. I have to admit, it was a rather clever way to avoid attention by attracting it first. I'll have to keep that in mind for the future, now that I have three dashing men following me around.

Since thick hedges are keeping us from simply walking into the area between the four pavilions where I assume the pond is located, we take to the roof. We could try and sneak through the building itself, but it's much safer to take the high road.

James runs off as soon as we start to scale the walls. I'm sure he'll find a quicker way to our destination. The urge to shift flows through my veins, but I push it down. This isn't the time. I'm not the size of a house cat; I'd stick out even more if I shifted than now in my assassin garb. Later, once we're done, I'll shift and go for a run, I promise myself.

Gryphon reaches the roof just before me.

"Are you okay?" he asks when I climb over the edge. "You're slower than usual."

"Usually I don't get poisoned and almost die."

"Fair point. Do you need a break?"

"In your dreams. Let's get there before we not only find a diamond, but also a body in the water."

We sneak across the flat roof, barely making a sound. I wish every roof were as flat and easy to traverse as this. When we reach the other side, we can finally see what's hidden in the centre of the pavilions. The pond is more of a small lake. Water lilies grow close to its banks. I sniff the air. Fish. If there are koi carp in the water, I'll grant myself an extra dose of catnip to celebrate my prophetic powers.

A stage has been built on the far side of the pond. A few servants and guards are scattered across the open space, but the guests are all still busy listening to boring speeches. Once again, I feel a tiny bit of pity for Lennox and Lara.

"I count seven guards," Gryphon whispers. "Did you see the woman?"

"No, and I can't smell her either. I wonder if she's run away rather than face the possibility of drowning."

"I wouldn't blame her. Do we use a distraction or shall we just try and sneak past the guards?"

A new scent hits my nose before I can reply. Benjamin. He's close. I turn in the direction of the scent, but I don't see him. I hope he hasn't spotted us. Luckily, I'm the only one with an extraordinary sense of smell.

"Benjamin is nearby," I warn Gryphon. "Be on your guard."

He nods. "Any sign of Ryker?"

"No, and the others are still among the guests. As long as we can evade Benjamin, we should be fine."

It's strange that we've not encountered Ryker yet. His cats must be keeping to their side of the bargain. I think he might be a little angry at them after. And at me. But that's fine, I can live with that, as long as I have a massive diamond in my pocket.

We climb down the wall and lightly drop onto the soft grass. It's nice not to land on stone as usual. Hedges and bushes line the side of the building, so we rush to the closest one and hide between it and the wall. I take a deep breath again, filtering the air for familiar scents. Still no sign of the woman nor of the rest of my team. This is too easy. I guess the challenge will be retrieving the diamond from a pond. Luckily, Gryphon doesn't mind getting wet. Or at least he doesn't mind it as much as I do.

A cat approaches us from my right. It's not James, but I recognise her from earlier. She's on our side. She sends me an image of Ryker eating a big chunk of gammon. Ah. So that's what he's up to. I grin. I should have known. We're very similar in that regard.

"Keep him occupied," I whisper. "The longer you can keep him away from here, the more catnip you'll get later."

The cat purrs and runs off before I can say anything else. I sigh and whistle. Three other cats come running, all of them part of James's troop.

"I need you to distract the guards," I tell them. "Try it by looking cute at first. If they don't react to that, harass them, attack them, whatever you want. Just make sure they're too busy to see what's going on at the pond."

A wave of glee rolls towards me. The cats are looking forward to manipulating the human guards. I shouldn't be surprised.

"Only stop when I whistle for you again, okay?"

All three of them bow their heads before running away, each of them in a different direction.

"I love cats so much," Gryphon sighs. "How did I get anything done without them?"

"I'm glad you love us. I hope you love me the most though."

He laughs and kisses me on the cheek. "Fishing for compliments?"

"No, fishing for diamonds. I can hear the guards fussing over the cats, so let's go while they're occupied."

We break the cover of the bushes and hurry towards the closest bank of the pond. The darkness is on our side; there are no lanterns close to the lake.

We kneel on the side of the pond and stay as still as possible while taking stock of the situation. The smell of fish has grown ever stronger, but I don't recognise the scent. It's not carp, that much is for sure. A new scent underlies the fishy smell. Blood.

"Kat?" Gryphon whispers. "Did the woman wear black shoes with golden buckles."

"Yes."

"Then I know where she's gone."

I turn to where he's pointing. Half a shoe pokes out from between large water lily leaves. The smell of blood makes sense now. Something's happened to the woman and I bet she didn't just drown. You don't bleed while drowning, unless you're really stupid.

"I think there's something in the water," Gryphon mutters ominously. "Maybe we should keep our distance."

"In case you've forgotten, there's a diamond in that pond, and we need the diamond to win this challenge."

"Is it worth being eaten for?"

I sigh. "We don't know if she was eaten. I can't see anything beneath the surface; the water is too murky."

"What could possibly be down there? Some kind of freshwater monster?" He dips his finger into the water. "Yes, it's not seawater. Are there even monsters that can live in a pond this size?"

I shrug. "I know as much as you do."

I whistle until a cat runs towards us. I hope no guard spotted him running across the lawn.

"I need you to fetch us some meat," I order. "As raw as possible. And no, you can't eat it. We need a whole piece, alright?"

The cat looks a little annoyed, but sends me a sense of affirmation, before he hurries away.

"Good thinking," Gryphon says. "I don't fancy holding my hand in to see what's lurking beneath the surface."

The sound of a twig snapping reaches me moments before a familiar scent hits my nose. Benjamin.

He's found us.

CHAPTER TWENTY-ONE

"Fancy seeing you here," the thief mutters and drops to the ground beside me. "Aren't you supposed to be in bed?"

I growl. "If you tell anyone that I'm here, I'm going to make sure you're tied to your own bed for the next three weeks. Understood?"

He holds up his hands. "Hey, I never planned on ratting you out. I was kind of expecting to see you here. It's not like you to stay at home, no matter how ill you are."

"I'm fine," I say automatically. "The poison's gone from my system."

Gryphon clears his throat. I glare at him and he decides not to say anything. Good boy. I'm perfectly healthy. I don't need people asking me if I'm okay all the time. It's getting tiresome.

"What have you found out so far?" I ask Benjamin.

"Since you're here, I assume the same as you. The diamond is in the pond. It took me forever to persuade a waitress to tell me that. She literally had her hands in my trousers-"

"I don't need to hear that," I interrupt. "Gross. You're my employee."

"You don't mind Lily telling her about her exploits," he protests.

"Yes, but Lily isn't a child. Plus she's half-succubus. Seducing people is in her blood. For you, not so much. Do you know anything else? Have you seen anyone who might also be after the diamond?"

"I've heard a lot of town gossip, more than I would have liked, but no, nothing that would help us. Why are you still here and not in the water, diving for the jewel?"

I point at the shoe. "Because someone else tried that and died. The water smells of her blood. We have no idea what's lurking inside the pond and we're not exactly willing to go in to find out."

The cat chooses that moment to return. Perfect. He carries a large piece of undercooked bacon. Even though I only just ate, my mouth waters at the smell. I would love to take a bite, but if the cat has managed to control himself, then so will I.

"Let's see if we can coax out whatever's in there," I mutter and rip the bacon into two halves. The cat looks up expectantly, but I'll have to disappoint him.

I throw a piece of bacon into the centre of the pond. It lands with a splash, followed by hundreds more splashes as the water begins to boil. Small fish tear at the meat, some of them jumping out of the water to get to a better position. The water's surface is one big battlefield.

"The pi'has are very active today," one of the guards says in the distance. I freeze, hoping we're hidden well enough by the darkness. A cat meows close to the guards.

"Yes, don't worry, I'll pet ya some more," the guard chuckles good-heartedly and a second later, the cat's contented purr reassures me that the human is once again distracted.

"Pi'has," Benjamin echoes. "Here, in Attenburgh."

"What are they?" I ask.

"Fish. Deadly fish. Blue-bellied pi'has are known for their bloodthirstiness. They eat anything and everything that they can get their jaws on, including each other. It's brilliant, really, using them to guard the diamond. Nobody will be able to get close without being torn apart."

I sigh. "If you remember, that includes us. Unless you know a way to pacify them?"

"No, I doubt there is one. They're controlled by nothing but their instincts, and if they tell them that there's food to be had, then they'll attack."

I turn to Gryphon. "Could you use your magic?"

"I'm not sure. I've never tried to influence anything less intelligent than a dog. And dogs are easy because they want to do what you're telling them anyway. Maybe we should find a way to raise the platform instead."

"That would immediately alarm the guards," I interject. "We'd need a massive distraction to keep them from noticing. No, we need to do this fast, before the speeches end."

Gryphon looks unhappy, but he nods. "I can try. Just don't be disappointed if this doesn't work."

"You'll do brilliantly," Benjamin says with his usual enthusiasm.

Gryphon raises his eyebrows at the thief, but then smooths his expression and stares at the pond. I cross my fingers and try to do the same with my toes. This has to work, otherwise we'll have to come up with a new plan, which will probably involve distractions, fighting and chasing. And it's no fun when it's us being chased and not us doing the chasing.

"Kat, tell the cats do be loud," Gryphon mutters as his brows furrow together in concentration. "I'll have to sing for this."

I nod and whistle in a pitch that humans can't hear. This time it's James who comes running. I'd love to know where he's been, but there's no time.

"We need a loud distraction," I tell him. "Right now. Start a fight or attack a guard, I don't care, but do it now."

He bows his head and disappears into the night.

"It's polite to say please and thank you," Benjamin whispers. "You should work on your manners."

I'm tempted to hit him, but back when I founded M.E.O.W. I vowed never to hurt my employees. It's hard to follow that self-imposed rule sometimes, especially when it comes to Bethany. Benjamin is usually the one who I'm never enticed to punish.

A loud crash in the distance almost makes me jump up. It sounds like about a hundred plates have all decided to commit suicide at the same time by tossing themselves onto the floor. Clever cats.

As I hoped, the guards run away towards the commotion, leaving the courtyard empty. As soon as they're gone, Gryphon starts humming. It starts as a familiar melody, one I've heard him use before, but then slowly changes when he begins to sing. I don't know how he does it, but even though he's singing, I can still hear the humming as an underlying melody. I don't understand siren magic and I likely never will. I doubt Gryphon knows himself how exactly it all works.

The water of the pond had calmed after the fish finished their meal, but now that Gryphon is singing, they're swimming to the surface, assembling in one big blueish mass. A shiver runs down my back. They're each no bigger than the palm of my hand, but their maws are almost half the size of their bodies, with razor-sharp teeth and jaws that look strong enough to bite through bone. There must be at least a hundred of them. No wonder the woman disappeared into nothing. I bet they've devoured every single bit of her, except for that one shoe that got stuck among the water lilies. I give a silent thanks to the nameless woman. If she hadn't been there, Gryphon would have gone into the water and suffered her fate.

The shiver moving over my skin turns colder. I could have lost him. That thought scares me to bits. Gryphon gone, taken within seconds, without me being able to do anything.

I grind my teeth and focus on the present, on his song. It's no use thinking of what could have been. It didn't happen and that's the most important part.

The siren changes his melody slightly and the fish move as one, drifting to the left until all of them are in one part of the pond, leaving a large space empty just in front of us.

Gryphon points at the piece of bacon I still hold in my hand.

"Want me to test it?" I ask to confirm.

He nods without stopping to sing.

Alrighty then. Let's hope this works.

I throw the bacon into the unoccupied part of the pond, close to where we are standing. A ripple runs through the swarm of pi'has, but none of them breaks away from the group. The meat slowly sinks to the ground of the pond, undisturbed by the fish.

I smile at Gryphon, but the grin leaves my lips when I realise how exhausting this is for him. It seems to be more difficult to control fish than humans. I suppose he has over a hundred minds to keep track off rather than just one or two. We need to hurry, that much is clear from the sweat pearling on his forehead.

The plan had been for Gryphon to dive down and retrieve the diamond, but he'll have to keep singing if this is to succeed. I look at Benjamin. If this doesn't work, if Gryphon loses control, could I live with the fact that I sent him to his death? No. I'll have to do it myself.

I look around one last time to make sure the guards haven't returned yet, before pulling off my boots and jumpsuit.

"Hey, some warning next time," Benjamin complains. "Some things are best left to the imagination, like your employer's boobs."

I ignore him. I'm wearing a bra so there are no boobs for him to see. Besides, I have more important things to think about than my nudity.

"Will you be able to hold them back for long enough?" I ask Gryphon.

He nods, but points at his watch. Time is of the essence.

"Alright. Don't mourn me if I get eaten."

I take a deep breath and step into the water. It's freezing. I'd love to stand here for a while to get used to the temperature, but instead, I wade away from the bank until the ground disappears beneath my feet and I'm forced to swim.

Urgh. I hate swimming. Especially in a pi'ha infested pond. Not my idea of fun, but a cat gotta do what a cat gotta do to get her claws on a diamond. No way am I going to just sell this after. I'm going to sleep with it in my arm in recognition of the trouble it took to retrieve it. And then I'll take it home to find a higher bidder than the person who told us about it in the first place.

Although I still want to meet them. I wonder if they knew how the diamond would be kept safe from ordinary thieves. No human would be able to distract the pi'has like

Gryphon is doing. A thought jumps into my mind. Maybe it was never about the diamond at all, but about getting rid of thieves and criminals. Only the best would be able to find their way here. The best, who are the biggest threat to society. They'd go into the pond, get eaten, leaving no trace of a struggle for the next poor sod to try the same.

It's a theory to think about more later, but first, I need to get the actual diamond. The water is too murky to see it from above the surface, so I'll have to dive. I throw one last look at Gryphon and Benjamin before disappearing in the pond.

Even my superior sight doesn't help in water brown with mud. The pi'has must have stirred up this soup. I'm blind and reliant on my sense of touch alone. I dive to the bottom, which isn't actually all that deep; maybe three metres from the surface.

I stretch out my hands and feel around the bottom. There needs to be a platform somewhere with the diamond on top of it. Instead of a gemstone, I find bones. I'm not a squeamish person, not in the slightest, but I even I shudder a little when I touch bone after bone. The unlucky souls who were eaten by the pi'has. I come across at least four skulls – one of them must belong to the woman from earlier – before I run out of air and have to resurface.

"Got it?" Benjamin shouts as soon as he spots me.

I shake my head, take a deep breath and dive again. It takes me three more goes until my hands finally push against something harder than bone. Thank goodness. I don't think Gryphon can control the fish for much longer.

The diamond is almost as tall as my lower arm. Fuck. That thing is going to be hard to hide on our way home. I never expected it to be this big. I'm not surprised that the jewellers want to split it into parts. Even if they were to break it into a hundred smaller diamonds, they'd still be worth a fortune each.

I'm starting to feel like we've bitten off more than we can chew. I take the diamond and swim to the surface. My legs strain at the effort it takes with the extra weight. I'm not a good swimmer, but luckily, this pond isn't deep.

As soon as I resurface, I notice how the mood has changed.

"Hello, sister." Caitlin stands next to Benjamin, her hands on her hips, looking furious. "I think you have some explaining to do."

CHAPTER TWENTY-TWO

I've never seen my sister look this furious. Her eyes are literally glowing with anger as she stares me down.

I wade out of the water, dripping wet and exhausted.

"Can we do this later? You can shout at me all you want when we're back home." I sigh. "Want to hold this rock while I get changed? I'm freezing."

Benjamin snatches it from me, then stumbles, surprised by the weight.

"That's one big diamond," he says without taking his gaze off the jewel. "How does one so large even exist?"

I put on my jumpsuit, wishing I had a towel. Leather isn't exactly absorbent, so I'll stay wet even while wearing clothes. My limbs are heavy with cold and exhaustion. I want to go to bed.

A cat meows and an image is flung into my mind.

"Quick, hide!" I hiss. "Lady Lara and Lennox are coming."

We run to the closest bushes, barely managing to all fit behind them. It was easier when it was just Gryphon and me.

"What are they doing here?" Benjamin whispers. "The speeches are still happening. Shouldn't the mayor stay with the guests?"

"That was the plan," Caitlin mutters. "I wonder what's going on. None of the guards has returned here either. It's how I knew something was up. They were all standing in a huddle, discussing amongst themselves the reasons why they were told not to go back to the courtyard."

Mmhm. Only someone in charge could have made them stay away. Someone like Lady Lara. The cogs in my brain are turning fast. It can't be. Can it?

The mayor and Lennox have reached the pond. She looks at it, then takes a grey device from her pocket. A hum travels through the ground as soon as she presses a button. Moments later, a metal square appears breaks through the surface of the pond. The platform, now empty.

I grin and look at the diamond in Benjamin's arms. We've done well.

"You can come out now!" Lady Lara shouts. The amusement in her voice is clear. "I know you're there."

Lennox looks incredibly uncomfortable. Has he told on us? No, I doubt that. He must be just as surprised at this turn of events as us.

"Kat, come out. It can only have been you."

Gryphon grabs my arm. "Don't."

I shake him off. "I need to know what this is all about. I need to know how she's involved."

I don't say it out loud, but I have to be sure that she is the person I thought her to be. The woman I like and admire.

"Stay hidden," I whisper. "Especially you, Benjamin. If something happens, run and get the diamond to safety."

Before he can reply, I stand up tall and walk away from the bushes' protection.

Lady Lara smiles. "I knew you were here. How did you do it?"

"Do what?" I ask innocently. "And why aren't you listening to boring speeches?"

"A wee birdie told me that something was happening here."

"A bird?"

She shrugs. "It sounds better than an alarm that was triggered as soon as the weight on the platform disappeared. I had it installed just in case, although until you joined the game, I doubted anyone would actually be able to steal it."

I can't help but stare at her. I don't believe what I'm hearing. What this implies.

"Come on, Kat, don't disappoint me. Use that brain of yours. Make the connection."

Lennox shoots me a confused look. He doesn't know yet. I do, though. At least I think I do. There's only one way to find out if I'm right.

"You set the challenge," I say slowly. "You sent the letter about this 'business opportunity of a lifetime'. It was you who created the riddles, who made sure only the best would ever come this far. And then you killed them. Yes, the fish did the actual killing, but it was you who sent these people to their deaths. How many were there?"

"I'm not sure how many actually made it this far," she says, her expression guarded. "We will find out when we drain the pond."

I stare at her. She talks about it without any emotion. I didn't take her as a cold-blooded killer. Ruthless to a certain degree, yes, but not a murderer.

"Oh, don't look at me like that, Kat. You don't believe

I sent innocents to their deaths? I didn't send the letters to just anyone. Only the worst criminals in Attenburgh. The ones who kill for sport, who threaten the security of this town. I didn't want small-time criminals to be harmed; those who steal because they don't see another way to survive. That's why I set the challenges and riddles. Only those with resources and experience would get this far."

I shake my head. "That's still not good enough."

"What do you want me to say? That I regret their deaths? Yes, maybe I do. But they are the criminals who were sent to kill me. Who have killed many, many good people, including some of my friends." Her expression changes for a fraction of a second, betraying her nonchalance. This isn't just a calculated political act. She's grieving. It's revenge. Now that I can understand.

"But why us?" Lennox asks, voicing my own thoughts. "Why employ Kat when you were planning to kill her?"

"I never wanted to kill her," Lady Lara protests. She looks me straight in the eye. "Believe me, Kat, I never had any intention of harming you. You were never even supposed to get the letter. I don't know how you came to have one, but I will investigate why my courier delivered one to you. I doubt it's a mistake, or a coincidence. I only realised that you might be involved when Lennox mentioned the diamond."

He looks at me sheepishly. "Sorry, slip of the tongue."

"Don't worry about it," I mutter. "It doesn't matter now."

"How did you get past the pi'has?" Lady Lara asks.

I glare at her. "None of your business. And just so you know, I'm keeping the diamond. And I quit."

"You can't do that," she protests.

"I can. The diamond was promised to us. I don't want to sell it. Not to you, anyway."

Lady Lara laughs, but it's not a happy sound. "I don't care about the diamond. I don't want you to quit your job. You're the most talented bodyguard I've ever had. I value your counsel and experience already, and you've only just started. I'm sorry you got hurt in my employ. I'm sorry you got mixed up in this deception. Please, will you give me another chance?"

Pride caresses my heart. I like it when people recognise that I'm good at what I do. But I can't let that influence my decision. Lady Lara may just be saying all that to keep me pacified and under her thumb. How can I believe anything she says from now on?

I sigh. "I'll think about it. I need some time to process this. If I decide to continue working for you, I'll let you know."

I turn and walk away without another look. Lennox follows me and takes my hand. I squeeze it, grateful not to be alone.

It's time to go home.

THE MOOD IS SOMBRE AS WE SIT IN THE LIVING ROOM, staring into our mugs. The diamond lies on the table, but none of us pays it any attention. It's no longer important. What matters is what to do next.

Ryker joined us on the way back, alerted by his cats. We sent another cat to fetch Lily. Now we're all gathered, sitting in silence. The tea Bethany has made is strong; just what I need right now.

"I can't believe it was the mayor all along," Lily says after a while. "How did we not see that?"

"Because there was nothing to see," I reply. "She hid her tracks well. And why would we have suspected the mayor of Attenburgh? It looked like it was organised by criminals. It would have been logical. Now, nothing makes sense anymore."

I'm so tired. Not just physically; mentally as well. Lara's betrayal hurts more than the poisoning. She could have killed me. Or worse, one of my team could have died. It doesn't matter that she didn't intend it to be specifically me. Right?

At the same time, are her methods so different from my own? I have killed hundreds of people. Not all of them were bad. I didn't ask questions. I just did the job, took the money and went on to the next one. But I'm not the mayor of a town. I'm an assassin; killing is my job. For Lady Lara to employ such methods is an entirely different thing. It's scary. What else is she up to? What else could she be planning?

Maybe, the only way to find out is to stay close to her. Become her confidante, get involved in her plans.

I shouldn't deceive myself. I want to keep working for her. I like her. And I like the money this job brings with it. Plus, I still haven't found any trace of my sister. She might be out there, suffering, and working in the mayor's office offers a chance to find her.

"You want to go back, don't you," Ryker says gently. It's not a question. He knows me too well.

I nod. "But I'm not sure if I can work for her if I can't trust her. M.E.O.W. works so well because we trust each other. Trust each other with our lives. I thought it could be the same with Lady Lara, but I doubt it will ever happen now."

"What did you find at the bottom of the pond?" Lily asks. "Were there bodies?"

"At least four. But to be fair, I don't know if they were

all killed today. There was nothing left but their bones, picked clean by the pi'has.

"We should get ourselves some of those pi'has," Bethany suggests. "They make great guards, even better than the cats. More lethal for certain."

"And where are you going to put them?" I roll my eyes. "Are you going to build a moat around our house?"

She shrugs. "If necessary. Either or, I'm going to buy myself an aquarium. I want to study one of those pi'has."

"Are they edible?" Benjamin asks.

"You're not going to eat my pets!" Bethany snaps. "I'm not eating yours either."

"That's because you can't eat cats. And don't you dare suggest our fawn is going to be dinner."

I groan and get up. I don't have the energy to listen to their bickering today.

"I need a shower. Let's all think about what's happened and how to proceed. We can talk again tomorrow, when we've had some sleep."

As one, my three guys get up, ready to follow me. I smile. I might not be having that shower on my own.

CHAPTER TWENTY-THREE

The morning sun bathes the bed in orange light. It warms my face, stroking my skin like a lover's touch. I push the blanket off my body to let the sun reach more of my skin. I'm naked. I don't usually sleep without clothes, but I must have been too tired last night to put them back on after the guys had taken them off me. I smile at the memory. They'd made me forget the events of the day. First in the shower, then in the bed.

I stretch, greedily soaking in the sunlight. The nights are getting longer already; soon winter will be knocking on the door. I've been told Attenburgh doesn't get as cold in winter, but we're yet to find out if that is true. I love playing in the snow as much as the next cat, but it makes leaving no tracks very difficult. I broke my wrist once falling off an icy roof, so ever since, I've been wary of running over roofs in the winter. I'm looking forward to using the fireplace in the living room though. We've not switched it on since we moved here, but once it gets colder, it will be a welcome feature. I'll have to send someone to collect wood or coal for it. Maybe dress the boys up in tight lumberjack shirts and enjoy the sight as they all walk around with their axes. A man with a plaid shirt and a sharp blade is rather sexy.

Gryphon snores loudly. I can't help but laugh. *That* wasn't very sexy.

I close my eyes again and enjoy just lying in bed, without having to get up for work, without anyone threatening me. Just me and the guys and the sun.

"You're naked."

I yawn and look at Ryker. "Yes?"

"You're never naked."

I chuckle. "I was naked last night. You took off my clothes yourself."

"Yes, but usually, you put them on again before falling asleep." He smiles. "I like seeing you naked."

"What a surprise. I would never have thought with the way you're devouring me with your eyes just now."

"I could devour you in other ways too." He flashes his teeth. "It would be the most delicious breakfast."

My insides clench at the innuendo. It seems like the perfect start to the day. Sun and sex.

I spread open my legs and give Ryker a wink. "Go have your breakfast."

WILLOW IS SPREAD OUT ON THE KITCHEN FLOOR, TAKING A nap. She wakes up when I open the fridge to stare at its emptiness. Our fridge is a black hole. No matter how much we buy, it's always gone immediately. Having dozens of hungry cats and several insatiable shifters doesn't help the situation. At least we can afford to buy more food now that I have a job and we have a giant diamond in our living room. I checked on it after coming downstairs. It's still on the coffee table like a large ornament. It's hard to believe we have something as valuable in our house. Lady Lara is the only one who knows we have it, and she didn't seem interested. By now, the Jewellers' Guild will be in uproar though. Heads will roll, suspects will be interviewed, guards will be sacked. All because of a pretty stone.

That's what it is, in the end. You can't eat a diamond. You can make jewellery from it, but again, having pretty earrings won't help you when you're starving. The one use I have for a diamond is making knives from it. I've heard that a diamond blade can cut through anything. The only problem is, a diamond can only be cut by another diamond, and we're fresh out of those.

The fawn yawns softly and gets to its feet. She's gained weight in the days I was unconscious, and its wounds have healed almost completely. Its fur is shinier now and its ribs less visible.

"Benjamin has been taking good care of you, hasn't he."

She rubs her head against my thigh. Aww. She likes me.

"What do deer eat?" I ask her. "Does anything in the fridge look appealing?"

She doesn't seem interested in the contents of the fridge. She's busy licking my leather trousers again and again.

"Don't worry, it wasn't one of your relatives," I mutter absentmindedly. "I think this is cow leather. Since you can't tell me what you want to eat, how about some catnip? Deer eat plants, right?"

She continues licking. Oh well. Catnip it is. Purely to make her happy, obviously. And if I take a little bit for myself...so be it.

By the time Lily finds us, I'm sitting cross-legged on the floor, the deer's head resting in my lap. She's sleeping, droned out on catnip, while I stare into space, musing about the beauty of the universe.

"Oh Kat," Lily tsks. "We've talked about this. No catnip for you, and especially not for Willow. It's not good for her."

"Who says that?"

"Benjamin. He's the expert; he's read up a lot on deer."

"He's just saying that to deprive me of catnip," I whine. "You always keep me away from it."

"Because then this happens. You get emotional and needy. Or you suddenly start painting the walls because 'they look better with rainbows'. Remember that?"

"They did look better," I mutter.

"That's not the point. Now get up, I have to talk to you."

"To me?"

"No, to the deer. Kat, you're being ridiculous. I'll make you a detox smoothie and then we'll talk. I need your advice."

"Advice? You? Mine?" The words all tumble into each other until they no longer make sense.

I stroke the fawn's head and wish someone would stroke mine. Sometimes, I wish I could shift into a house cat rather than a panther. I'd be able to lie on someone's lap, purr and manipulate them into stroking me. Instead, people run away from me when I approach them. No head scratches for me.

"Why are you looking sad?" Lily asks.

"Because nobody is scratching my head."

She laughs. "Yup, you need my smoothie. Go to the living room and lie down for a bit until I'm done. I can't believe you've done this again."

"Willow was hungry," I protest, but she's already pulling me to my feet and pushes me out of the kitchen.

"Benjamin!" she shouts from behind me. "Your deer has been drugged!"

I ignore her and go to the living room as instructed. I give the diamond a little pat before lying down on the sofa. Life is wonderful.

* * * * * *

AFTER TWO GLASSES OF LILY'S MIRACLE SMOOTHIE, I CAN think clearly again. More or less.

Lily sits on the sofa opposite me, fidgeting and clearly on edge.

"Spit it out. What's the matter?"

She bites her bottom lip. "You know the man I used to get into the ball yesterday?"

I nod. "Yes, you said he was some rich high society guy."

"That's what I thought. A rich human. But I think he may be more than that."

My smile disappears. "Please don't tell me that he's a siren."

Lily doesn't meet my eyes. "I think he may be. I'm not sure. He doesn't look like one; it's why I chose him in the first place. He's got wrinkles and crow's feet and a scar beneath his right eye. He's not pretty enough to be a siren, but I think he tried to use his powers on me yesterday."

"You *think*?"

"It could have been someone else in the room, but he looked at me after as if he was surprised. He must have tried to make me do something, but of course that didn't work on me."

I lean forward, more than just intrigued by that siren. I'm worried. Was it just a coincidence that Lily met a siren who had tickets for the ball? Or could this be connected to the siren who attacked me?

Maybe I'm becoming paranoid. I know there are lots of sirens living in Attenburgh and most of them will be in positions of power. It could just be a coincidence. It has to be.

"And there's something else," Lily mutters, still not looking at me. "When the cat came to give me the agreed sign that it was time to leave, he smiled at it. As if he wasn't surprised to have a cat walk into a room full of people and head straight to me. I would have ignored the first bit but when I saw that look in his eyes, as if he was satisfied with himself, I knew I had to tell you."

"A siren who tried to charm you," I muse. "He must not have been aware that you're not human, but most people don't, so that's not surprising. Even if someone really did their research on M.E.O.W., they'd never know. Hell, I didn't know until you told me. I had my suspicions, but I wasn't even sure if succubi really exist."

"Well, now he knows that I'm not human," she sighs. "Or at least not fully. I just wish I knew what he wanted to make me do. Was it something as simple as making me kiss him? Or something a lot more sinister?"

"The only way to find out is if we confront him. Do you know where he lives?"

She shakes her head. "We always met in restaurants and hotels. He said he travels a lot for business and only has a small property here in Attenburgh, which is too small to entertain guests."

"Luckily, we're good at finding people," I say with a reassuring smile. "What's his name?"

She winces. "He called himself Peter Tamari, but I wouldn't know if that is his real name. At the ball, everyone seemed to know him, but they only called him Sir, never by his name."

The mystery deepens. As if we didn't have enough to do already. I need to find my sister, yet something else always gets in the way. Being poisoned was a good excuse for pausing the search, but can I justify putting resources on identifying this siren rather than looking for my own flesh and blood?

"You said one of the cats came to fetch you. Do you know which one?"

"One of Ryker's, I think she came to Attenburgh with us. Could be a he, it's not like I can tell them apart." She scoffs. "We should give them all collars with name badges."

I tense and her eyes widen.

"Sorry. No collars. Definitely no collars. Why were you asking about the cat?"

"Because they may have got the siren's scent and could lead us to him."

CHAPTER TWENTY-FOUR

Lennox joins me in the living room after Lily rushed off to Ryker to identify the cat. Lennox is wearing nothing but a bathrobe. One of the sleeves has slipped down so far that his shoulder and part of his chest is exposed. I'm tempted to reach out and run my hands over his skin, but no, that would only end up with both of us naked. Again. I've got work to do and can't let myself be distracted. Maybe I shouldn't have chosen three mates. Three of them means three times the potential of not getting anything done.

"Have you had breakfast yet?" he asks me.

"In a way." I grin. "I had some catnip and then two detox smoothies."

"That bad?"

I shrug. "It's been worse. Felt great though. I wish Lily hadn't caught me."

"It's probably good that she did. We need you rational and thinking straight after all that happened yesterday. Have you come to a decision yet? About the mayor?"

"Maybe." I sigh. "I think I'm going to give her another

chance. Not just because I like her and I like her money, but because I might find K7 that way."

"Good call. I would have recommended the same. We should have a talk with her, though, or at least you should. Lay all the cards on the table. She needs to tell you what other schemes she might have planned. If she can trust you with her life, then she'll also have to trust you with her secrets."

"I like that sentence. I think I'm going to steal it."

"A good thief doesn't announce his plans."

I laugh. "Which is why Benjamin is our thief. If you see him later, he may complain about me, by the way."

"Why?"

"I may have given his fawn catnip."

Lennox roars with laughing. "Oh Kat, that is so you."

"Of course it's me. I'm me. I do *me* things. Just like you do *you* things."

"Are you sure the detox smoothie worked? You still seem a little weird."

I flash him a grin. "I'm always weird. It's part of my charm."

The doorbell interrupts our bantering. I sigh. There's always something. None of the others is nearby, and Lennox is in his bathrobe (and I don't want anyone else to see his pretty chest), so it falls to me to open the door.

"I'll get dressed," Lennox calls after me. "Unless you want me to stay like this?"

I ignore him. I'm still surprised neither him nor Gryphon joined Ryker and I this morning. They were awake, but they didn't move, didn't say anything. They just listened. Weirdos. I bet it turned them on.

I look through the peephole and step back in surprise. It's Lady Lara. On her own. She must have walked here. Crazy woman. She's the mayor; she shouldn't be walking through half the city without guards.

I run my hands through my hair in an effort to tame my mane. I'm in my house clothes; a loose shirt and even looser trousers. Not what I'd usually wear in her presence, but this is my turf. She came to me so she can't expect me to be dressed for the occasion.

With one last deep breath, I open the door.

"Good morning," she greets me. "Sorry for coming unannounced, but I thought it was important to talk to you in person."

"Ehm...morning." I hate that she's so polite. I want a confrontation; I want to shout at her until she understands how disappointed I am in her. Now that she's here in person, last night's anger is bubbling up in me again.

"Come in," I say and turn away before I lose my restraint. I don't take her to the living room to talk, but to my office. I feel like I have the upper hand here. It's my official space for conducting business. Here, I'm the one behind the desk, even if it's not as nice as hers. I might use some of the diamond money to get a pretty desk. Walnut, I think, with a nice marble texture. Big enough to keep all my files on it and still have space to write, but not too big as to make me look small.

"Nice office," Lady Lara remarks.

I motion her to sit on the only other chair in the room. It's even squeakier than the one I'm sitting on.

I cross my arms in front of my chest and wait for her to say something. It was her idea to come here, after all.

"I wasn't sure if I should come here or not," she begins after a moment of silence. "I wanted to give you space, but I also felt like I didn't do very well in explaining myself last night. I didn't want you to get the wrong impression of why I did what I did."

I don't reply, waiting for her to continue.

She licks her lips; a strangely beautiful movement. "Four years ago, I was in a relationship with a fellow politician. We were both part of the town council. We were young, idealistic and ambitious. We wanted to change the world. Back then, the council was even more conservative than it is now. She only got in because of her parents, while it had been mostly luck for me that my mentor passed away and I was allowed to take on his role to maintain stability. Still, we thought we were invincible. We'd made it into the council and we were going to make sure that they changed for the better." She grimaces. "Of course, it didn't happen that way. First, they threatened us. Small threats at first, anonymous letters, dog poo through the letterbox. Then they left a dead squirrel on my doorstep. I would have thought it to be the present of a stray cat if it hadn't been for the noose around its tiny neck. It was a message that we ignored. And then they killed her."

My throat constricts. She's opening up to me, laying herself bare. I don't know what to do, so I stay silent.

"They made it look like a robbery gone wrong, but I knew it had been an assassination. That's when I started looking into Attenburgh's underworld. I needed to know what kind of people lived in my city. How they could do what they did to my partner. The longer I looked, the clearer the picture became in my head. There were several layers in that world below ordinary society, ranging from common pickpockets to master criminals. But the important thing I saw was that there were tendrils reaching up all the way to the richest people in town. They were the ones pulling the strings. That's the day I vowed to cut those connections."

"It's not just here where it's like that," I say quietly. "It was the same in my hometown. Poor people can't afford assassins. It's always the rich people who give the orders. They can afford to have others killed. Ordinary men might punch you in the gut. Rich men will send someone to cut your throat."

"And it shouldn't be like that anywhere," Lady Lara exclaims passionately. "We shouldn't have to live in fear of assassins. After my partner's death, I tried to find ways to stop Attenburgh's most powerful people from communicating with the underworld. It didn't work, of course not. They were far too resourceful. I decided that the only way would be to carve out the system from the bottom. Get rid of the assassins. Like I told you yesterday, I don't mind the general lowlife. Every city has those. I even try to help them with initiatives to offer more jobs and improve living standards in the poor parts of town. Education is one of my passions. If we reach the next generation, teach them how to make an honest living, we'll have a safer and juster society."

"Grand words," I scoff, suddenly angry again. "But did you ever think that not every assassin chose their profession? Some are forced into becoming killers. It's not their choice."

Her gaze softens. "Like yourself?"

"Maybe. Point is, you can't just kill criminals, no matter what they've done. They deserve a chance to defend themselves. Have a trial. Be proven guilty or innocent. If you stand above the law and take matters into your own hands, then you're no better than the people in the council you tried to change."

Her eyes widen, but then she nods. "You're right. I know that. I got so obsessed with the idea of drawing out the biggest criminals in town that I lost sight of my original aim. The pi'has were a bad idea, I admit that. I should have had guards lie in wait to arrest whoever tried to steal the diamond."

"Your tune has changed very quickly overnight," I reply. I want to believe her, I really do, but I don't know if I can.

"That's because the change of mind had already begun. I just didn't have the strength to change my plan. You won't know this, but I started putting this plan into action six months ago. To call it off at the last minute would have been the honourable thing to do, but it would have felt too much like giving in. Especially after you were almost killed. It was yet another sign of other people trying to influence my decisions by using violence." She sighs. "And in return, I resorted to violence myself. I see that. I know it's wrong. But sometimes, it looks like there's no other way. Those willing to hurt others will always be stronger. How can we stand against them without raising arms ourselves?"

"You're asking the wrong person. I'm not a pacifist. I kill people for a living. The difference between us is that I'm not the mayor. I'm not in a position of power. I don't have to be a role model. Nobody cares what I do, whether I'm alive or not."

"I do," she interrupts. "Don't ask me why, but I care."

I raise an eyebrow at her curious interjection. "Why?"

Lady Lara smirks. "You don't like following the rules, don't you."

"Neither do you."

"Which is why we're made for each other. I want you to come back and work for me. Not as my bodyguard, but as my advisor. You know your way around the darker sides of the city, but you've not lost your humanity. You'll be able to hold me accountable, unlike my other advisors who grovel at whatever I say."

Advisor. I mull the word over in my mind. It's got a better ring to it than guard. An advisor needs a brain as well as brawn. I'd be able to use all the skills I've learned while running M.E.O.W., while earning better money and doing something good at the same time. I scoff at my own thought. *Something good.* Since when have I wanted to do that? It must be an aftereffect of the catnip, or maybe the poison.

I take a deep breath. "I have several conditions if you want me to take the job."

Her expression brightens and she leans forward expectantly. "Tell me."

"First, you trust me with anything that relates not only to your safety, but mine and that of my team. That includes the cats. Second, you'll offer positions to all the other members of M.E.O.W. It's their choice whether to accept the offer or not. Third, complete honesty. Both ways. I get to know everything you plan, everything you're doing as part of your job. Private lives are excluded, obviously. And finally, I need your resources to find someone."

"Yes to the first three," she says without hesitation. "Who is that someone?"

"My sister. She's only a child, but I've been told that she's here in this city. Against her will. This might involve powerful people. Sirens. They've messed with my family before and we destroyed them back home. I'm willing to do the same here, if necessary."

"Trust me, I have no problem with you killing every single siren in this city," she says, her lips curled in distaste. "Ever since I found out they exist, I've realised how deeply they're embedded in our society. They're everywhere, pulling the strings from the shadows, or openly displaying their power as members of the rich and famous. You have any help I can offer to get your sister back."

I can't help but let out a relieved sigh. Finally, I might be getting somewhere. With Lady Lara's help, finding K7 should be possible. And to her plan of killing all the sirens...

"Not every siren," I tell her. "Since we discussed honesty, one of my partners is a siren. He's on our side though, you can trust him."

She looks surprised, but nods after a moment of silence. "If you trust him, then I will do the same. When I said 'every', I didn't mean it in the literal sense. I know there are exceptions in any species. He's the first good siren I've come across, but I'm willing to accept that he's not the only one."

"Kat!" Ryker shouts from the other side of the house. "We've got a problem."

I exchange a look with the mayor. "I'll be right back."

She smiles at me. "Don't worry, it's time for me to leave anyway. We can continue our conversation on Monday at work. Trust me, I'm glad we sorted this out."

She looks like she's about to hug me, so I quickly leave the room, letting her follow me. Let's not get too close after all that's happened.

Ryker is standing in the hallway, a black cat with brown paws by his side.

"Lily told me to find the cat who came to fetch her yesterday. This is him. And he's just told me that he can smell the siren nearby."

I gape at him. "Our siren? Lily's siren?"

"A siren?" Lady Lara asks sharply.

"I'll explain later. How close is he?"

"We should be able to see him if we go outside. But do we want to do that, that's the question."

"Where's Gryphon?" I ask.

"Out shopping, together with Bethany and Benjamin."

Fuck. One thing I learned about confronting sirens is that it's always good to have a friendly siren on your side.

"Alright. This might be our only chance to catch him. Get the others. We're going hunting."

He smiles, but doesn't look convinced.

"Why is he here, Kat? How does he know where we live? I doubt this is a coincidence."

The cat meows with urgently.

"He's getting closer," Ryker translates. "He's coming here."

I nod. We need to act fast. I whistle sharply, alerting every cat in the vicinity of the emergency. They start running towards us from all sides, their paws light on the ground but still audible to my shifter senses. At least ten of them were inside the house. Wow, I hadn't realised that.

"Lily! Lennox! Caitlin!" I shout at the top of my voice.

I especially need Lily to come and identify the siren as the man from the ball. The cat may have remembered the wrong scent, who knows.

The others arrive in seconds. Thank goodness. Lennox is still in his bathrobe and shoots me an apologetic smile. I guess he never made it to the bedroom to get changed. Caitlin looks like she's just got out of bed. Her hair is all over the place.

"What's up?" she asks with a yawn. "What's the emergency?"

"The siren is outside, approaching the house," Ryker explains and points at the peephole. "Lily, take a look. Is it him?"

Lily takes one look, and freezes.

"Kat, don't go out there," she whispers. "Don't look."

"What's wrong?" I growl, worry transforming into anger.

"It's him, but he's not alone."

I can't hold back any longer. I push her out of the way and press my face against the door. A man stands on the other side of the street, a large cart behind him, and on his side, a child.

I don't think. I only react.

I open the door so fast that it slams against the wall.

"Kat!" Lily shouts, but I ignore her. Ignore all of them even as they try to stop me from running outside.

The girl stands motionless next to the siren. Mottled, dirty hair hides most of her face but I know without a grain of doubt that it's her. K7. My sister.

"No closer," the siren warns as I sprint towards him.

The threat swinging in his tone makes me stop in my tracks.

"Finally we meet in person, K1. It's a pleasure," he says smoothly, reminding me of a snake wrapping around her prey.

"My name is Kat," I hiss. "Now hand over my sister."

He laughs. "I believe there's something of a misunderstanding." He grabs the tarp covering the cart behind him and yanks on it. It falls to the ground, revealing a cage. He's brought a cage with him. Did he transport my sister in it?

Rage fills me, turning my insides into molten lava. I press my fingernails into the palms of my hands to stop myself from lunging at him. I can't endanger my sister, not now when I've finally found her. She still hasn't moved. Hasn't acknowledged my presence.

"Step into the cage."

The siren's voice is as cold his heart.

I sneer. "And why on Earth would I do that?"

In a flash, he draws a knife and holds it against my sister's throat.

"That's why."

For the first time, she lifts her head. I look into her eyes; bottomless pits of pain and suffering.

The world stops turning. My heart stops. Everything just stops.

And I walk into the cage, ignoring the shouts and cries of those I leave behind.

For my sister.

✿ ✿ ✿ ✿ ✿ ✿

The End

✿ ✿ ✿ ✿ ✿

Meow! What a cliffhanger! Sorry about that (or not).
The story continues in Claw, the sixth book in the series. To get updates about the Catnip Assassins and other books, subscribe to my newsletter.

Kat would also like to encourage you to leave a review. Don't tempt her to sharpen her knives. She's scary that way.

ABOUT THE AUTHOR

Skye MacKinnon is a USA Today & International Bestselling Author whose books are filled with strong heroines who don't have to choose.

She embraces her Scottishness with fantastical Scottish settings and a dash of mythology, no matter if she's writing about Celtic gods, cat shifters, or the streets of Edinburgh.

When she's not typing away at her favourite cafe, Skye loves dried mango, as much exotic tea as she can squeeze into her cupboards, and being covered in pet hair by her two bunnies, Emma and Darwin.

Support her on Patreon and get exclusive benefits:
patreon.com/skyemackinnon

Subscribe to her newsletter:
skyemackinnon.com/newsletter

facebook.com/skyemackinnonauthor

twitter.com/skye_mackinnon

instagram.com/skyemackinnonauthor

bookbub.com/authors/skye-mackinnon

goodreads.com/SkyeMacKinnon

amazon.com/author/skye_mackinnon

www.ingramcontent.com/pod-product-compliance
Lightning Source LLC
Chambersburg PA
CBHW030632190726
48286CB00008B/2496